To

Dear
Cindy ,

Best Wishes

Shilo Gupta

Book Review

Each page is a masterpiece, perfectly encapsulating the tone of the book and adding to the brilliant pacing of the book. The author has crafted suspenseful moments, developed the different characters' personality traits and revealed their dark secrets. All the details play into each other and the entire plot becomes so complex. The timing of each word and chapter are masterfully placed. The narrative goes back in time, switching perspectives, which add to the twist to the story. The end was so shocking – all the pieces woven together intricately and make the story to be exactly what you think, it wouldn't be.

I would highly recommend this book to anyone who wants to read an exceptional book that cannot be put down till the whole mystery is solved. Excellent attempt for a maiden novel!

— Anurag Yadav

ISBN: 978-0-9984833-1-3

Sun Publishing LLC
27 Riesling Court, Commack NY 11725 USA
Enquiry: info@sunpublish.com
Phone: +1 631 455 3677
www.sunpublish.com

Managing Editor: Sangeeta Gadhok Magan
Cover Design: Sunil Koli
Cover image provided by Shalini Gupta
Print: Kamal Printers

TROUBLED WATERS

"A FICTIONAL NOVEL BASED ON IMMIGRANT LIFE IN AMERICA"

SHALINI GUPTA

Dedicated to

the memory of my mother

Mrs. Krishna Mahajan,

who in spite of her tiny frame

possessed limitless strength.

ACKNOWLEDGEMENTS

This book would not be possible without the support of my husband and my children who have always encouraged me to write. My husband has openly liked my writing and my children have done so grudgingly.

Much thanks are owed to my dear friends, who offered to give this book its first read and provided constructive criticism.

The editorial guidance provided by Sangeeta Gadhok Magan from Sun Publishing helped in providing shape to the final draft.

The greatest thanks, however, belong to the reader who has committed to read this book and provide the ultimate indulgence for the writer.

Shalini Gupta

PROLOGUE

This book should be read just as a story; maybe a horrifying story unfolding from poorly treated mental illness in the background of immigrant life in America.

I will not wax eloquent on the necessity of recognizing mental illness and treating it, as there are many existing platforms for that. I will definitely not theorize about offering any unique perspective into the immigrant experience in America as millions of people have lived, breathed and relished it before me and will continue to knit their own stories into this vast and complicated fabric that we call America.

As an immigrant from India settled in America, myself, I have often remarked jokingly to my friends that only a crazy person would leave their motherland, and then try to assimilate into a diametrically foreign culture and live to tell the tale.

My real reason for writing this book was merely to tell an Indian story unfolding within the multicultural strands of American society, a story of imperfect characters, haunted by the lives they chose to create. Immigration is not without emotional consequence. First-generation immigrants, whether they immigrated from what is now known as Pakistan (Anand) or India (Kunal and Maya), are cultural orphans as they juggle between different values and norms. Their line between right and wrong gets fuzzier with every moral dilemma they face. Their points of reference shift constantly as they try to set their own set of norms. They shift and resize their religious rules to fit their hectic lifestyles. They make decisions relevant to the here and now. They do things that would be unacceptable to their ancestral roots. They break traditions and reshape the cultural molds at their convenience. They try to survive and excel and rationalize their way onto financially successful lives. Eventually, they work hard, succeed beyond their own expectations and should achieve happiness. The looming question is do they?

CONTENTS

CHAPTER ONE

SHOCK AND AWE . . .
JANUARY 2013

It was a cold and windy day. The clouds were large and thick and blanketed the evening sky in a peculiar and dark gloominess. There was a hint of snowflakes forming in the air. They were pure, light, feathery and beautiful. They floated and fell dreamily onto the windshield of his Mercedes Benz and disappeared within seconds, dying away with the swish of windshield wipers, leaving an ugly brown slush on the edges.

"How can a pure and beautiful snowflake turn so ugly within a few seconds? Just like my life," thought Kunal, with a grunt.

Almost subconsciously, he turned the wipers on high, trying to wipe the ugliness of the slushy snow *and* his life, away from his thoughts.

He drove on slowly, ruminating and occasionally swearing to himself under his breath every time his car skidded in the now thickening snow.

The landscape surrounding him was still so foreign to him. More than thirty years in this country and he felt as if he still did not belong here.

"There is nothing that I can truly call my own here, other than my checkbook," he thought wryly, muffling a deprecating laugh.

The buildings that he drove by, the slippery roads, even his car seemed foreign to him. He turned his attention to the car radio. The weatherman was preaching about the inclement weather followed by uninspiring commercials about a furniture store going out of business. Soon the radio chatter merged into a meaningless cluster of words spraying upon his numbing consciousness. He shut the radio off angrily.

The drive today was darker and drearier than usual.

As he turned into his gated community there was not a single car to be seen on the street, and an inconsolable feeling of complete loneliness came over him.

He had no particular interest in going home today. He did not want to linger at work either. His employees were heading home to their families. He tried to imagine their lives.

His manager having dinner with his family, listening to the kids' chatter, the wife's smiling welcome leading most certainly to an array of nagging complaints, followed by a short argument easily resolved, *"Seriously! Who wants to fight at the end of a freakishly tiring day?",* then settling in to watch their favorite tv show and sleep, already preparing ahead for the next day.

Kunal, on the other hand, had nothing to look forward to except a dark house, a disloyal wife, dinner eaten alone in his bed and yet another sleepless night spent with disquieting thoughts in his head: thoughts with multiple voices that were getting louder and more violent each day.

"This nasty half-dream is bound to end," he consoled himself.

He wished for a godly power to wave a magic wand and make the ugliness go away. He wished to be awakened into a different life in which everything would be back to normal. A tiny voice in his head reminded him continuously that this was not a dream, that there was no magic wand and things were *never* going back to normal.

This nightmare was all too real, and it was here to stay.

He wondered why he should feel so bad this time. It was not the first time that this had happened. His wife, Maya, had cheated on him before and he had been able to get over it. He had gone through the necessary steps: counseling, confrontation, anger, grief (not in the same order) and had moved on. On those occasions, he had immersed himself in his work, stayed in his office longer, even slept in his office when he felt like it. He had worked extra hard on those occasions and had very effectively converted his sorrow into dollars.

He had always recovered from these truant episodes of hers.

"Bless her whoring heart, she has given me enough practice, I would say," he wiped his brow as he ruminated.

He had arrived at his house; his letterbox was in front of him, but he did not turn into his driveway. He stepped on the accelerator and kept on driving further away from his brick faced colonial with cathedral ceilings.

He was not ready to go home just yet.

He continued with his reverie, muttering to himself occasionally, driving mindlessly and turning uselessly onto strange streets.

This time, her truancy had hit him harder than before. He could not seem to shake this one off as easily. His brain was strangely numb, as if a paralysis was spreading over his senses and encapsulating his mind.

He tried to remember what his therapist had told him. He tried to recollect the coping mechanisms that she had taught him; take deep breaths, count to 100, think happy thoughts.

He tried replaying pleasant memories in his mind, but his vision was repeatedly captured by the ugly slush collecting on his windshield. With each swish of the blades, he imagined drops of blood, Maya's blood, mixing with the muddy sludge at the edges. In the middle of the windshield, right in front of his eyes, he saw a blurred, hazy image of Maya's face bleeding slowly, getting paler by the second. He was oddly attracted to that apparition, and he held on to the hallucination, reveling in its ghostly justice.

A flashing red traffic light shook him out of his trance. A quick return to reality harshly whipped his fantasy away.

He was not able to relax. His fists were clenched around the steering wheel and his veins were popping up now, like dull blue serpents crawling underneath his skin.

"This is not going to be easy," Kunal thought.

It was not going to be just a hard day; it would more likely be a hard six months.

That was about the time it took for him to recover every time he got upset at her.

He kept on driving. His mind swung between violent fantasy and reality. His temples were now beginning to ache from a slow, gentle throb.

CHAPTER TWO

DEVIL WOMAN . . .
SPRING 1993

Kunal knew very well that Maya, his wife of thirty-odd years, had cheated on him on multiple occasions.

The very first incident was devastating for him.

It was five years after their marriage. Their son, Sonu, was three years old. She had told him that she was going to watch a movie with her girlfriends. The babysitter had already been arranged, she told him, and he would not have to hurry back from his important meeting.

His meeting was in a downtown banquet hall at the Ritz Carlton. He had parked as close to the entrance as possible, so that he could quickly dash in, run to the elevators and race to the boardroom on the fifth floor. He was going to meet with the city council. Some of the biggest names in construction business in town were going to be there. He was extremely excited for his project: a movie theater in an upcoming local strip mall.

If he got this contract, they would be rich soon!

As he was parking, he saw Maya's car. It was parked a few spaces away. He was shocked and confused, staring at her car in utter disbelief. With trembling hands, he called her from his cell phone. She answered right away and reminded him that she was at the movie theater with her friends and will be home later.

Kunal missed his meeting. He parked his car further away, stayed in his car and waited…for *three hours!!*

As if a lifetime later, he saw Maya emerge from the hotel with a well-dressed white man. He saw them kiss lightly and wave goodbye and head to their respective cars. He ducked in his seat hiding himself from her view, as she drove past him.

In his rearview mirror, he watched her cautiously as she drove away.

He was shaken to the core. He remembered that scene vividly. He could recall each sordid detail with chilling clarity.

He was overcome with dread, lightheadedness and a sickening wave of violent nausea. His palms were sweating, his face flushed, he began to hyperventilate and gasped for air. He felt as if he was choking in his own shame, as if he had been publicly stripped naked in front of a cheering crowd. The filthiness of his wife's morality crystallized in front of his eyes and his stomach churned, making him taste his own bile in his mouth. His heart raced uncontrollably, a million violent thoughts danced in front of his glazed eyes until he retched and threw up in his car.

In the following days, he wished that he could scream at her at the top of his voice and let her know what he thought of her. He could neither talk to her, nor look her in the eye. He could not confront her. His embarrassment on being taken for a fool was too great. He started avoiding her for hours at a stretch.

It was almost ridiculous. He was acting as if *he was the one who had cheated on her!*

He knew that the situation had to be addressed. However, he could not bring himself to talk to her. He was too angry. In his mind's eye, she was covered with filth. Just the mere sight of her made him heave violently.

He avoided looking at her to the point of banishing her existence altogether. Slowly, over the next few weeks, she ceased to exist for him. His mind had reduced her to just a shadow walking around his house, *a silhouette with no face*. That was the only way he could cope with his errant wife.

His manner grew increasingly belligerent and defiant towards her. He slammed doors and swore constantly at no one in particular. He walked around the house with a strange defeated look in his eyes. His mood grew darker and darker. He was staying at work longer. He was starting to drink again. He appeared gloomy all the time.

The only time Maya saw Kunal smile was when he played with Sonu, deriving great joy from his childish antics. He was overindulging him and openly spoiling Sonu; buying expensive gifts, bending over backwards to fulfil any wish that Sonu expressed.

Kunal's angry silence towards Maya lengthened and eventually stretched to a total of six months.

There was no change in *her* behavior, though. She was unaware of what was going on in his head. She did not know that he frequently fantasized about hitting her head with her favorite paperweight *just to see her blood seep into a tiny puddle underneath her.*

Maya was trying to bring things back to normalcy as she suspected that something was deeply wrong. She suggested that they should have friends over, Kunal refused to meet them. She tried to make plans for evenings out but had to constantly cancel them as Kunal failed to reach home at the expected time. Maya was trying really hard to win Kunal back: she cooked his favorite foods, played his favorite music; even watched his favorite movies on DVD. All these efforts were proving futile.

One day, Maya told Kunal that she was going to have a few people over for their wedding anniversary celebration. He started laughing in a sinister fashion. No words came out of his mouth which was by now hidden behind a thick beard, only an ugly jeering maniacal laugh as he pointed at her. He still remembered the quizzical, worried, afraid look on her face as she left the room, scared.

"Anniversary party, ha! Got to give her points for a poignant sense of humor!", he thought putridly.

Kunal did not show up for the party *at all,* leaving her to be embarrassed in front of her friends. He stayed at work all night and even slept in the office. He returned home at 8 am in the next morning.

She was waiting at the door when he entered the house.

Boy, did she lose her temper that day!

The truth came out in the fight that followed. Kunal remembered the shouting match that culminated in Maya's frustrated sobbing, her shaking voice drowned by his loud accusations.

He told her that he had seen her leave the hotel with a man.

Maya's face became white and beads of sweat appeared on her forehead instantly. Till this day, Kunal remembered the look of complete bewilderment on her shamed face with sadistic pleasure.

"YOU WERE WITH HIM, WHEN YOU WERE SUPPOSED TO BE WATCHING A MOVIE WITH YOUR FRIENDS!

WHO THE HELL IS HE?

YOU ARE HAVING AN AFFAIR?

YOU TRAMP... YOU DIRTY WHORE..."

She said that she was sorry.

She had met that man at a bar where she had gone with her friends.

She swore on her son's life that she has never ever been unfaithful to him before.

She would move heaven and earth and she would make it up to him.

Of course, she loved only him.

Of course, he was the best husband she could hope for.

Of course, she was happy with her life.

Of course, this would never happen again.

Of course, he did not trust her anymore.

EVER.

Maya and Kunal sought marriage counseling and dutifully saw a counselor in the following weeks. They were taught techniques for coping with stress and for better communication between each other. They were counseled regarding techniques to resolve conflicts. They were advised to practice using words and actions which would not be hurtful. They were instructed to attend weekly sessions and to work towards the common goal of being tolerant and loving to each other.

Maya and Kunal worked on the suggestions and instead of meaninglessly fighting all the time, they were able to be polite and considerate to each other. Kunal, especially, fully co-operated with the suggestions from the counselor.

According to the therapist, the marital counseling worked! Maya and Kunal stayed in the marriage and worked at their goal of having a happy future.

However, in Kunal's heart there was no love left for Maya. Inwardly, he continued to stay hostile towards her. Loving her, after her adultery, was not even a remote possibility in his mind.

"That ship has sailed for good."

Kunal just did not care enough in his heart to make matters any better.

On occasion, his mood worsened to the point that it affected him physically. He had to be hospitalized with chest pains and was diagnosed with acute *stress reaction.* He was advised to seek the help of a psychiatrist and was diagnosed with adjustment disorder and was prescribed antidepressants. For his episodes of *rage reactions,* he was placed on mood stabilizers.

He did not take any of his medications as prescribed, nor did he tell the psychiatrist about his hallucinations and violent thoughts.

Maya and Kunal stayed cordial to each other. If Kunal had any questions about her fidelity, he kept them to himself. He did not probe too deep; he really did not want to know. He stayed distant from her so that there would be no failed expectations.

Why had he stayed married to Maya?

Kunal had many answers to this question. Most of the reasons were cultural.

The major reason was devoid of all pragmatism: he believed he still *loved* her. He could really not imagine his life without Maya.

Indian upbringing had ingrained in his mind that marriage was a permanent, religious and a lifelong bond, not a mere legal contract. Getting divorced would be like venturing into unchartered waters. He had never known a divorced couple. None of his immediate family members, aunts, uncles, cousins or friends were divorced.

American society was different. Divorce was not unusual among married couples, young or old. Lately, divorce rate in Indian marriages was creeping up as well here. Still, it was a foreign concept for Kunal.

Kunal theorized that if he stayed married, his son Sonu, would have a stable family life. A divorce would be detrimental to Sonu. Kunal firmly believed that children from divorced households suffered from adverse psychological effects that impacted their future lives unfavorably. For the sake of his son, he would never consider a divorce. Maya might be an unfaithful and a disloyal wife, but she was unquestionably an exceptional mother. He was willing to live this life as long as Sonu had a good mother.

Yes, the only reason that he was staying in this marriage was his son.

He did not want to seek a divorce even though he was unhappy in the marriage. He wanted to continue with his life and leave things exactly the way they were.

His business on the other hand, *flourished. He* worked harder than he ever had in his whole life. His bank balance grew by leaps and bounds and looking at his bank statements, his mood improved each passing month. If he were ever asked the secret of his success, he would have happily explained: *a strong mental jolt that his wife had delivered him would motivate anyone to pour their entire time and effort into work!*

Years and years of living this pathetic, perverted life had turned Kunal into a bona fide *workaholic.* He had become an expert at avoiding Maya's existence altogether. Each passing day, he immersed himself deeper into his work.

There were times, when he wanted to be able to trust her again. He wanted to free his mind from constant doubt and disbelief. However hard he tried, he was not able to bring himself to love neither trust Maya.

Nothing in his life, however, could have prepared him for today. His *darling wife of so many years* had managed to deliver yet another blow that had shattered him to the very core.

CHAPTER THREE

JANUARY 2013 CONTD . . .

Kunal had seen Maya earlier this morning. She was busy with her morning paper, reading glasses on, looking up at him with those indulgent eyes, smiling at him. She was calmly sipping her morning cup of coffee.

(One spoon each of sugar and cream; he knew how she took her coffee.)

He grabbed his bowl of cereal and pretended to be in a hurry when he was not. He was trying to avoid her, run away from her as fast as he could, *as usual.*

Kunal was still at the table, when she headed upstairs to shower.

He had accidentally picked up her phone from the counter. They had the same phones (as part of Sprint family plan!!). He needed to call his secretary to schedule a site visit. As he started to dial the number, he saw the messages.

"Remember, our flight is at 2:30 pm."

"Where are you? I am glad that you have finally decided. Have you told him? I hope you have. Be safe, though. I do not want him to lash out at you."

"See you tomorrow."

She had not told him about any trip.

"Is she running around with another boyfriend now?"

"What was she hiding?"

"WHAT??"

Intense rage had overcome his senses. He left her phone on the kitchen counter and sped to his office. His heart was racing, and a wave of nausea came over him. He wanted to run before he did something to hurt her. His hands seemed to be *dirty and vile* merely from touching her phone. He wanted to run away and wash his hands instantly, with a strong soap. He wanted to run outside and draw a deep breath, to cleanse his lungs from the same air that *she* had breathed.

He wanted to just be as far away from her as possible.

Kunal entered his office, muttering an inaudible response to the chirpy "Good Morning, Sir" to his secretary, Lisa. He hurried past her without so much as looking at her and stepped into the hallway, leading to his desk by the window.

He canceled his meeting, worked absentmindedly at nothing in particular, scribbling half-heartedly at a blueprint that he was drawing up for his next project.

After two hours, Lisa tapped at his door looking rather uncomfortable as she handed him the large envelope.

"This envelope just arrived from a lawyer's office and your signature is needed on the receipt."

Worry furrowed Kunal's brow as he peeled himself away from his disjointed thoughts. He quickly signed at the dotted line. He opened the envelope hurriedly. In pure disbelief, he read the notice from a *divorce attorney*. As he opened the envelope, he recognized a smaller envelope inside with Maya's handwriting on it.

Sure enough, it was addressed to him.

"Dear Kunal,
I have been meaning to tell you that I am ending our marriage.
We both know that we are unhappy.
I do not see myself living this sort of life any further.
You have been a good provider and a great father.
Sonu is now older and is doing well in college.
I take the blame for our unsuccessful marriage. I know that you have never forgiven me. Of course, too much time has passed now to make amends.
I am planning to move out of town, soon.
Take care.
Maya"

Kunal's hands were sweaty and shaking. He felt that there was not enough air in the room. He had to get out and get some fresh air.

He just had to get away.

He wanted to ask someone what *he* had done wrong?

Wasn't he the one who had done everything right?

Wasn't he the one who was cheated on?

Wasn't he the victim here?

Wasn't he the one who sacrificed his life by staying in the marriage for the sake of his son and the society?

Hadn't he been humiliated enough already?

Now this....?

"God alone knows who she is going away with," Kunal thought bitterly.

He read her note again and again. She was right, though, in more ways than one. Of course, he had never forgiven her.

How can you forgive a cheating wife?

Isn't it enough to make a living, provide every possible comfort, always put family first?

The vapors of pure hatred had swelled up like a hissing cloud of steam in his mind.

After the initial shock had passed, he almost felt relieved that she was leaving him. Maybe now, there would be an end to this distasteful way of living. Now, he did not have to pretend any more. His friends would eventually understand. His son Sonu would be fine. He is older, now (*as she had said rightly in the note*).

He read her note again.

Actually, she was pretty much right about everything that she had mentioned in the note!!!!

Never in his life had he agreed with her more...!!

He got in the car and left his office. On his way, he stopped at the gas station to pick up a pack of Marlboros. He had not smoked in twenty years, but today he felt like a smoke.

Whenever Kunal thought of Maya, he felt as if he was in the presence of *pure evil*. He felt something snap in his mind. He felt terrified and oppressed by the very thought of her.

Once again, the urge to run away as far as possible, overcame him. He was worried that the evil emanating from her would pierce his soul and make a home in his heart. He had to get away.

Kunal was also worried that he might *do* something to hurt her. Her calm face from this morning appeared in front of his vision.

He wanted to take an axe and split her head open right down the middle of her skull with one sharp stroke.

He got back in his car and drove around for a while. He decided to call his son, Sonu in San Francisco, just to take his mind off his turbulent thoughts. Sonu was just waking up.

"Dad, did you forget again? There is a three-hour time difference between us! Where are you calling me from? Let me call you later."

He joked with his son, asked him how he was, how his second semester at Stanford was coming along. It was good to hear his voice. His son's voice calmed Kunal's feeling of rising dread and panic.

Generally, phone calls with Sonu lasted longer. Sonu, in spite of his generous allowance was always short of money. He used these phone calls very successfully to extract money from his overindulgent father.

Today, he seemed to be in a hurry to get off the phone.

Today, he did not ask for money, which really struck Kunal as extremely unusual.

Kunal was unashamedly proud of Suneet (nick named Sonu) his young, handsome son, who had the rakish good looks that Kunal once possessed in his *younger days.*

A million years ago...

After his phone call with Sonu, he calmed down a little bit. His car automatically turned towards the Hindu temple, the local temple where he had not gone for fifteen years. He went in, a little unsure of how to pray again. He wanted some peace and quiet, and a divine intervention which would make those terrible thoughts in his head go away.

He prayed and prayed, repeating the one prayer song that he remembered from his childhood. He wished that the gods in the temple could save him from the gathering storm in his mind. He wanted the priest to give him the holy water that would cool the throbbing headache encompassing his temples. He was willing to do any penance, pay any price to buy some relief from the disquiet in his soul.

But all that failed.

Kunal was not able to get the evil darkness out of his head. In his mind there seemed to be only two images flashing repeatedly.

The first image was his head slamming into the wall again and again until he had no further thoughts in his head.

The second image was of Maya's skull splitting into two parts, with a single stroke of a sharp axe until blood splattered everywhere, leaving her face lifeless.

Kunal left the temple and started driving again, towards his home. However, each time he reached his house, he drove past, into his silent neighborhood, loosely circling an everchanging route.

Snow was starting to fall rapidly now. Thick snowflakes crowded his windshield, as he fell back into his thoughts. His mind grew numb and frozen, just like the frigid landscape that surrounded him. He kept on driving meaninglessly, losing track of time, letting his mind wander.

He drove all night. When he felt sleepy, he pulled into a gas station and slept for an hour. The bitter cold awoke him, and he started his car. He started driving again and when he saw the sign for McDonald's, he pulled into their drive-through and ordered a large coffee and a muffin.

The steaming hot coffee helped him think again. He waited till it was 8 am and called his office to cancel his appointments for the coming week.

He continued with the wandering ruminations of his mind, remembering events at will, at times going into minute details of his memories and at times dismissing the details.

He drove on aimlessly, the harsh daylight bothering his sleepless eyes.

CHAPTER FOUR

SOMETHING IN THE AIR . . . 1984

It was a sunny, pleasant day in the month of June 1984. The manicured grounds in the campus at the DCA (Delhi College of Architecture) were teeming with students.

They had chosen a common dorm room and had finally settled in. Today, they were clustered outside the assembly hall, anxiously taking notes of all sorts of information displayed on the notice board. Maya and her friends were excitedly checking the schedule for upcoming classes.

It was a chatty group; each girl was talking animatedly about something important. As is common with a group of girls, there was definitely more talking and hardly any listening going on! There was apprehension and exuberance in the air. Many concerns were being expressed regarding the beginning of the new college year; many questions were being asked and answered. Most of the talk was pertaining to the subject of choosing the classes for the first student year.

They were all proud of being selected to study Architecture at this prestigious institute. Admission to DCA was not easy and only the meritorious few were accepted as students every year. There was loud nervous laughter that mixed in periodically with the general noise. Occasionally, a glimpse of uncertainty could be detected in the eyes of these future young architects. The next four years were going to be life changing for the entire group.

Maya's eyes were scanning the grounds when she saw Kunal. He caught her looking at him and came and stood next to her, eagerly introducing himself with a handshake.

"Hi, I am Kunal, Kunal Sinha, " he said as he looked straight into her eyes.

"Or Konal, " she smiled and pointed at the misspelt name on his badge.

He laughed shortly as he followed her gaze to his faulty badge.

He was a transfer student and had transferred from Mumbai School of Architecture. *(She had already seen his name on the list of transferred students).*

"Who does that?" she had thought to herself. *"I would give anything to live in Mumbai as compared to New Delhi. "*

He looked unkempt, unshaven and carelessly dressed. If he was going for the shabby, hippie look, Kunal Sinha was *surely* nailing it that day! Every time she looked in his direction, her eye lingered on the misspelt name on his badge.

He was her partner in the Architectural Graphics and Design course, he informed her. He laughed briefly, a nervous laugh, and kept looking into her eyes, unblinking. It seemed as if he could not peel his eyes away from her.

Her friends had teased her mercilessly about the effect she had on boys. Her eyes were like giant magnets and boys could not resist the force of attraction that was exerted by them. They laughingly mimicked how boys made excuses to talk to her just so that they could look into her eyes. They also imitated the frightening glare that Maya gave a boy if he ever dared ask her out on a date.

Kunal's voice was well cultured and she was impressed by his handshake.

When he stood closer to her to peer at the notice board to look at his class schedule, that brief favorable impression was replaced by a wave of *sheer revulsion*. Involuntarily, her nose wrinkled up at the strong stench that emanated from his unwashed body covered with unwashed clothes.

"Gosh, you skipped on your shower today, didn't you?" she said almost involuntarily. Normally, she would not be so rude, but the boy *really needed* a shower!

"Well, I shower, sometimes," he grinned, still holding her hand, which she wanted to reclaim in a hurry.

"Oh, I am sorry," He hurriedly let go of her hand.

"My luggage got misplaced in the flight from Mumbai. The airline is going to send me my suitcase probably by tomorrow. Hopefully, then I can shower and change into clean clothes and smell better."

For the rest of the day, she kept her distance because the body odor was definitely a deterrent.

The next day he was still stinky. Maya pointed out to him that there were clothes and soap that could be bought in New Delhi, with a little effort and a small amount of money.

He just looked at her and laughed.

On the third day, her partner was clean shaven, barbered, and in a new set of clothes and he smelt good, to her relief. Actually, she admitted to herself, he was rather handsome.

"Wow! What a transformation? What is this cologne?" she asked.

"Old Spice, nothing special", he smiled back at her. *"I'm glad you do not have the same expression on your face today."*

"What expression?"

"Well, the **I am about to vomit***, expression!"*

"Ha-ha! The truth is, I cannot stand body odor. We can both agree that you smelt no better than something out of a pigsty for the last two days, but you do clean up good!"

From that moment on they were always together. Maya and Kunal worked on their assignments together, they hung out with the same group of friends and they studied for exams together.

Yet, they did not consider themselves an exclusive couple as they had not gone on a date.

They were spending so much time with each other that Maya's friends assumed that they were romantically involved. When they started teasing her about it, Maya was furious with them for indicating that they were in *love* with each other.

However, after five months, the thought that he should have asked her out by now, *if he fancied her at all,* started preying on Maya's mind.

"Why hasn't he asked me out so far?"

"Am I not pretty enough?"

"Am I not up to His Majesty's standard?"
"Am I fat?"
"Am I short?"
"Am I ugly?"

Days flew rapidly and weeks and months passed, and he had still not asked her out. By the end of the year, it had become a cause for major concern for Maya. Something had to be done and she decided to enlist her able friends to help her in this matter.

Hours were spent on why he had not asked her out so far. All explanations were entertained ranging from the most probable to outlandishly outrageous ones.

"He may be brilliant and good looking, but he is gay."

"He is *mentally retarded*. Does he not see how beautiful you are and how lucky he is that you even agree to be with him."

"He has *erectile dysfunction.*"

"He has a girlfriend back home in Mumbai"

"He is married."

"He is just not into you."

"For sure *he* is gay."

"Maybe *you* are gay."

Finally, when Valentine's Day came and went without any further progress, it was decided that a strategic intervention was needed to resolve the issue.

She was with her five best friends: Sandy, Lata, Kavita, Mandy and Neeti. A plan was made and would be immediately put in action. If it worked, it would definitely ignite a fire in Mr Kunal Sinha's brain processes and as a result he would either:

go crazy with jealousy
or
give in and ask her out.

The plan was smooth, was simple and had been tried multiple times in the past and needless to say, was always known to work. The major requirement for the plan was to invoke the power of jealousy and combine that with a good measure of manipulation and enticement.

"Maya is to pay no further attention to Kunal anymore, starting tomorrow. Rather, she will smile generously at Saurabh (an equally good looker, but insufferable because of his lack of intelligence, a good sacrificial lamb, nonetheless)."

"We know that Saurabh already likes Maya. He will love to be with her. Saurabh and Maya will be seen together everywhere and by that we mean everywhere: the cafeteria, the library, the cultural center etc. Then, Mr. Slowpoke i.e. Kunal will become jealous and he will have to take the next step and ask Maya on a date. and then everything will fall in place," Sandy outlined it all with the seriousness of a lawmaker and the cunningness which can only be ascribed to a madam running a brothel.

The plan was put in action the very next day. Brilliant as it was, it would have worked too, but for a major flaw.

There was no Kunal.

He had to rush back to Mumbai for a family emergency. His mother was extremely sick, and he had taken the evening flight the previous day.

He did not return for the next fifteen days.

CHAPTER FIVE

THE SPOT
IN THE SUN . . . 1986

When he finally returned from Mumbai, Kunal had deep shadows under his eyes. His mother had improved now and was out of the hospital, he told Maya.

He had become very quiet and he had a fatigued look about him. It appeared as if he had brought the pain and suffering borne by his mother back with him. His eyes were devoid of all light and there was a deep silence in place of his amiable smile. Every time Maya tried to talk to him about his mother's illness, he shook his head and walked away. He could not bring himself to talk about it at all.

It seemed to Maya that Kunal had aged from that trip. He was a different person, changed in his outlook and behavior. His mother's illness had obviously affected him deeply. He wanted to be left alone most of the time. He did not hang out with her or her friends as much. She saw him every day and they worked together in the lab. However, there were no attempts at flirting or exchanging knowing smiles anymore.

He appeared so serious and lost that Maya's *sinister* plan to make him jealous and coax him into asking her out was never put into action.

Over the next four years, Kunal made multiple trips to visit his mother as she had repeated bouts of illness and hospitalization. Each trip tattooed a new expression of sadness and hopelessness into his face. He had started sporting a beard and looked older, worried and haggard. He had started keeping more to himself and was seen less and less with Maya and her friends.

He was mostly seen with Akshay, a senior, who was from the same city as Kunal.

Rumor had it that Kunal had started drinking, *heavily.*

Maya was very unhappy. There was no laughter or joy left anymore. Kunal's pain was everywhere and she could do nothing about it. She could not bring a smile to his face anymore. His eyes looked at her with a dark tired stare.

At times, it appeared to her that Kunal was trying to break free from the shackles of pain that held his spirit captive, as if he wanted to laugh, even if just for a moment but, invariably, an invisible shadow stifled his mood, and he was submerged into deep gloom again.

He was trapped in sadness. There was a wall stronger than steel around him and Maya was powerless in breaking it down. She just could not reach him, however hard she tried. He was hurting; she could see that, but there seemed to be no easy way to soothe that hurt. He was just not willing to talk, and it was hard to bridge the growing gap between them.

Her friends mentioned that Kunal was deeply depressed and he should seek treatment. Maya grew increasingly concerned. She wanted to intervene and help him; she truly did, but each time she tried to talk to him, he avoided her. She felt as if she was banging her head against a brick wall.

"How can I help? He wouldn't even talk to me. Whenever I try to talk to him, he walks away. I know that he is depressed, he should really see a doctor. It is so frustrating."

Yet, Maya vowed to keep on trying and convince Kunal to seek help. If the grapevine was to be believed, Kunal had also started smoking in addition to drinking.

Maya spent most of her time worrying about Kunal.

CHAPTER SIX

I CAN DO WITHOUT THE
PAIN . . . 1987

Kunal was drifting, aimlessly. Anything that could distract him from his mother's struggling face was a welcome respite. Drinking eased his mind and softened the harsh days into a mellow blur of events. He had also started smoking. His mind craved the calm and quiet that the first pull from a cigarette provided and alcohol served as a very successful sleep aid.

Also, he was making more and more friends!

It was amazing to see how many new friends he had now. Ever since word got around that he had a ready supply of alcohol and a stash of cigarettes, he was never alone in his room. Money was always scarce for most of the students and Kunal Sinha came from a rich family. The prospect of free booze and cigarettes was surely a crowd pleaser and fellow students buzzed in and out of his room.

His mother's health was declining with every passing day. His father had sought the best treatment for her epilepsy, consulted with the best doctors in Mumbai, yet she was steadily deteriorating.

Each time Kunal went home, his mother was admitted to the hospital. He saw her tied to the bed rails until her seizures were controlled. Every visit depressed him and lately, he was finding it harder to cope. He was helpless: nothing he could do would make her healthy, and it broke his heart to see her slipping away.

Kunal's heart was fraught with worry and despair and he could not bring himself out of the dark cloud enveloping him. The hopelessness of his mother's illness combined with his depression affected his sleep and he was getting nightmares. At times, he dreamt that he was drowning; his limbs thrashing meaninglessly in an attempt to rise up for air but falling short with every try. He just could not break through the surface to breathe.

How he wished that his mother was healthy and did not have to face her physical struggle every day!

Only time when he forgot his worries was when he was in his room *drinking* or in the library—studying.

The booze also helped him forget Maya.

"How madly had he fallen in love with her!"

"How could he ever make her a part of his life? How could he ask her to marry her and bring her into his sordidly depressing home because of his mother's ugly uncontrollable disease?"

Maya was a beautiful girl and his soulmate. However, he did not want to drag her into his nightmare. He had dreamt of marrying her, but now his dream was overshadowed by the image of his mother's ugly episodes of seizures, and vomit frothing at her mouth. Introducing Maya to the contorted face of his mother covered in vomit, was a forbiddingly unpleasant thought for Kunal.

More importantly, Kunal wanted Maya to see his mother as the sweet, affectionate woman that she was. It was hard for any stranger to look past the ugliness of her epilepsy. All they could see was a helpless soul trapped inside the merciless grip of an uncontrollable disease. They could not appreciate her beauty or her loving heart when they saw her.

Maya wouldn't understand, she *couldn't*. She *couldn't* look beyond his mother's physical disease. She *couldn't* realize that his mother was not just a patient but an exceptionally loving person. She *couldn't* look beyond her disease when she saw her... just like everybody else *couldn't!*

Moreover, he was not sure that he wanted to share this pain with her.

It was his pain, his cross to bear.

There was absolutely no reason for Maya to be any part of it.

Kunal wished that he could explain all this to Maya. He had tried speaking to her on the phone, but he could not bring himself to speak at all and had to put the phone down. Those occasions had only made him drink more and made his mood even darker.

He realized that he was in a very dark place. His life seemed joyless, devoid of all hope and the shadow of his mother's death lurked around every corner of his imagination. Every time he called home to talk to his father, he worried that something terrible had happened to his mother.

Each passing day, Kunal's burden lay heavier on his mind. Either he was studying hard, or he was drinking in his room and brooding. Sometimes, he wondered how he survived when he was not drinking. He knew it was a bad habit, but he needed a crutch right now. He was not planning on becoming an alcoholic, he just needed the peace and calm alcohol offered his troubled mind, *just* for now.

Slowly but surely, with the help of alcohol, he was reducing Maya to an irrelevant blur. The more he drank, the less he saw of her. Every day that Kunal spent widening the distance between her also meant that he did not have to share the ugly, embarrassing truth about his mother's illness with Maya.

He had once fancied marrying Maya as he had regarded her as his soulmate, not just a girlfriend.

Now, the very thought of planning a future with Maya *terrified* him.

CHAPTER SEVEN

MY HEART WILL GO ON . . . 1987

Maya felt as if she had just been on a brief roller coaster ride. Kunal had come into her life as a pleasant breeze and then got lost in a thick mist through which she could barely catch a glimpse of him.

Gone was the friendly face of a carefree boy that she had met on the campus grounds two years ago. Now, Kunal was bearded, unkempt and visibly depressed. He shifted his gaze away from her whenever she looked in his direction. They had not spoken for a year and a half.

It was as if he had built a glass wall around him. She could see him but try as she might, she could not reach him.

Even though Kunal had shunned her from his life, she could not bring herself to hate him.

She had fallen in love with him. It was a simple enough scenario in *her* mind. They were two young persons in love, studying at a prestigious institution. They would soon be professionals in a respected field. Their entire future was ahead of them. They could do anything they wanted.

However, Kunal had estranged himself from her. He was depressed and was caught in a swamp of sadness. She wanted to rescue him. However, he was unreachable, impervious to all her efforts to help him.

After many failed attempts to talk to him, she had no choice but to let him go, and just wait.

That was all she could do!

The *sinister* plan hatched by Maya's friends for quick starting Kunal into proposing, by using Saurabh as a sacrificial lamb, was never put in action. There could never be anyone other than Kunal in her life.

Two more years passed.

In her final year, Maya was shocked to hear that Kunal's mother had passed away. Kunal had not been seen on campus for two months. Maya tried calling him again, but he never picked up his phone. She sent him a letter, writing for him to call her if he wanted to talk.

He never called. He never wrote back.

Maya decided that she had done all that she could do.

Maybe, they were not meant to be together.

There must be a reason why he shunned her so passionately. With tears stifling her resolve, she declared Kunal to be a closed chapter in her life.

The final exams were approaching. She decided to focus on her studies and got busy preparing for the exams. With the hectic studying schedule and endless cramming that had to be done for the exams, Kunal became a mere shadow in her mind as well. She was a good student and when needed, she could summon up immense concentration to blot out everything from her mind other than studies. The task at hand was to ace the finals and everything else had to take a back seat to that.

Occasionally, she worried about Kunal; how he was going to pass his exams after such devastating news.

CHAPTER EIGHT

MOVING ON . . . 1988

Kunal's grades did not suffer much. Surprisingly, he was one of the top scorers in his class.

When exam season came, he was found glued to his books. During those days, he was a permanent fixture at the library and stayed there from six o'clock in the morning until it closed. He read all the architectural textbooks from cover to cover. He felt a strange peace when he was in the library. Studying architecture soothed his trouble mind, a feeling that was duplicated only by being extremely - *drunk.*

Kunal often thanked God that his father had not forced him to join his successful accounting firm. Many of his friends had ended up joining their family businesses. They had not even had the chance to pursue their own dreams regarding their future career and had expressed their misgivings to Kunal on multiple occasions.

Kunal had no aptitude or attraction for a career in accounting and his father had respected that. Architectural Design was his passion and would be the perfect profession for him. It provided him the opportunity to be creative and was challenging in a purely cerebral manner.

His dream was to be a great architect and make a name for himself by designing buildings that would reflect the future. He wanted to be recognized not only for unique style but also for environment-friendly energy solutions to be utilized in commercial buildings. His style was very geometric, modern and sleek. In his dreams he had imagined many skyscrapers uniquely different from anything that the world had seen so far.

Books transported him into another world. While studying, he was relieved, even if briefly, from the ache that crushed his chest continually.

The exams were finally over.

Maya had done extremely well.

So had Kunal!

There was a sense of relief on the entire campus.

No more late nights studying!

No more overdoses of caffeine!

No more sleepless nightmares of failing the exams!

There was different kind of buzz in the campus. Everyone was busy making their resumes. Job applications were a hot topic and campus job interviews were the talk of the day. The future was fast becoming a tangible reality for the fresh, young and hopeful architects.

In the Girls' Hostel however, there was a different topic for discussion in every room. The *parents* had started looking for prospective grooms for their freshly qualified daughters. Marriage proposals were the burning topic of conversation. The prospect of being sought after by many *suitable boys*, added a special coy smile to the young faces.

Maya's main worry at this time was—*packing!* The room had to be vacated by the end of the week and the impossible task of packing up her entire life into two suitcases had to be accomplished.

She was going home to her parent's house.

Her parents were going to activate the process of *arranged marriage* as soon as she reached home. They would want her to look at certain *boys* that they had shortlisted for her. This was the most dreaded period in any girls' life. The *parents* were the ones in charge now. *They* will let you know who the right person was for *you* to spend your entire life with. This idea reeked of a stench worse than a raw sewage pond.

Decidedly, *arranged marriage* was a bitter pill to swallow. However, millions of women had gone through this before her and, (she consoled herself) it would not kill her, either.

Or so she thought!

CHAPTER NINE

SAVE ME . . . 1988

"Maya beti is home," her dad announced in his booming voice as Maya entered the house.

"Janaki, Maya is home!"

Her mother came out of her kitchen where she had been cooking Maya's favorite foods especially for her. The smell of all the spices hit her nostrils. Her mother smiled happily as she came out of the kitchen wiping her brow on her sari.

After the initial hugs and kisses, it was time to eat.

For Maya's mother, life revolved completely around food.

"As long as there was food to eat, there could be nothing wrong with the world!" was her motto.

For Maya, it was great to be home. It was wonderful to sleep in her childhood bed, leaf through her cherished old books, listen to her music, and eat food and snacks that her mother prepared while sipping countless cups of tea.

"*If I kept on eating like this, I going to get fat!*" thought Maya.

After a few days of this indulgent treatment, the novelty wore off. The unhappiness that Maya had brought home with her resurfaced out of the shadows and cast a dark spell on her thoughts again. Kunal's face was constantly in front of her eyes again and her recently broken heart ached all over again.

There was another nightmare to be dealt with. From now on, Maya had to participate in the sport of *"arranged marriage."* It had consumed her parents' imagination ever since she had joined college. Every waking thought they had, was about how to get their daughter married to a suitable boy.

Her mother brought out a folder that she had started for this purpose. In this folder, neatly arranged, was all the information regarding multiple prospective grooms for her. It was comical to see how much time and effort her mother had put into creating and maintaining that folder.

As Maya had dreaded, she had to become a part of this *circus,* whether she liked it or not.

Each morning started with her mother opening the big folder. Almost every week they were meeting a new family, a new prospective groom.

"*And this one is a doctor,*" her mom screamed excitedly, one day.

Maya went through the motions, got dressed up, met the families and the "*excellent boys*" *(as her father liked to call them!).* After they left, the next week was spent discussing the pros and cons of that particular *rishta.*

Maya was running out of excuses to reject the *excellent boys* as her future husbands.

Maya's appetite and sleep were getting affected. She could not blot out Kunal's face from her mind. About a million times the thought of contacting him came to her mind, but the memory of the defiant and listless look in his eyes deterred her from doing that.

She called her best friends to compare notes. Each one of them was going through the same *circus* and facing the same conundrum. Some were happy and excited. It was surely awkward they told her, but once they finalized the groom to be, it was mostly fun.

They talked about all the gifts they had received, the shopping they had done, various trips to the tailors and the jewelers, the preparations for the ceremonies pertaining to the upcoming *WEDDING*. They asked her to call them if she needed help. They could tell her about the best stores for bridal wear, jewelry, and shoes. They would also willingly give Maya advice about makeup, hair and honeymoon destinations.

Invariably, the talk ended with the insecurity of an uncertain future that faced them. They would cease to exist as carefree daughters raised indulgently by adoring parents. Soon, they would have to assume the roles of brides, wives, daughters-in-law, sisters-in-law etc.. The most difficult part of all this, they all agreed, was having to deal with the *mother-in-law*.

"And how are you doing, Maya?"

She could not bring herself to share the state of her mind and her sadness in her heart when her friends were so jubilant.

After the meeting with the "*doctor*" (*who was from a very decent family, an excellent, excellent boy!*) and his rejection by Maya, her parents sat her down at the dining table.

"*What is it Maya?*" asked her mother. "*Why are you doing this to us? We have shown you so many suitable matches and you have not liked a single one of them.*"

"*Is there some boy that you like?*" asked her father.

She burst into tears and went to her room.

Her mother followed her into the room. She sat down next to her, held her hand and worriedly asked her, "*What's wrong, Maya?*"

"*Oh, don't worry,*" Maya said. "*I'm getting a little overwhelmed. Ever since I have been home this meeting the boy, getting ready, going out with strange people that I may have to spend the rest of my life with is getting to me. I am sure this was not easy for you when you had to go through this.*"

"*I understand,*" said Maya's mother, empathetically. "*In my time, we did not have many choices. I finished high school and got married. We did not have boyfriends, or love marriage like you people do now. I don't think I have done too badly for myself. I have a nice husband, a nice family and that's what life is all about.*"

"*I guess I just need some more time. Can I have a little break from all this for the next few days?*"

"*Yes sure. Anyways, the next person that we were going to meet with studied at the same college as you, some Kunal Sinha. His father has contacted us many times over the phone and they want to meet, but I'll call them tomorrow and will ask them to cancel for now.*"

"*Oh, really. REALLY? Can I see the folder please?*" Maya cried.

Her heart was beating fast, as if it would thump right out of her chest. She dared not allow herself to smile, until she was sure that it was *him*.

*"Let's face it! Kunal is a pretty common name. But how many Kunal Sinhas could there **be** in my college? Not that many!"*

Maya's mother brought her the folder. There, attached to the biodata, was *Kunal's* picture. It was not really a great picture. It made him look more like an employee applying for a job.

His beard was gone, *thankfully*.

More importantly, it was definitely him!

"Do you know him?" asked her mother quizzically.

Suddenly, Maya was happy, and a big smile broke onto her face as she nodded.

It seemed to Janaki that her daughter had finally come home!

CHAPTER TEN

SURPRISE, SURPRISE . . . 1988

Maya's happiness knew no bounds when she saw Kunal's picture in her mother's dreaded yet meticulous folder. Her mother had quickly surmised that they were more than just classmates. She had spoken to her husband to contact Kunal's father. Kunal's father had called right back and arranged for the meeting in the next 3 days.

She was happy to see that Maya was taking more interest in this *rishta*. Maya herself was helping with the preparations this time. She was helping with setting up the house. She was busy cleaning and throwing away junk that her parents had collected in the house. She was even planning the menu for dinner that day. She went shopping and got new clothes for herself.

"All these are good signs," thought a very relieved Janaki.

As was customary with this stage of matrimonial venture, the initial meeting was at the house where much honor and thanks were bestowed upon the *boy's* family. A lot of small talk was made and the traditional introductions between the various aunts and uncles from the *girl's side* and the *boy's side.*

It almost seemed like the warmup to a friendly cricket match between India and Pakistan, if such a thing could ever happen!

Eventually, a decision was made by the elders that the *boy and girl* should be allowed to be with each other for a few minutes for having *soft drinks or coffee.*

The only thing that seemed to bother Janaki was the fact that both Kunal and his father were men of few words. Kunal's mother had recently passed away just about six months ago. He was the only child in the family. There were barely any women in their family. Kunal had an aunt, his father's sister who had settled in Australia. She was not able to visit them until the wedding.

She noticed that both of them appeared to be enveloped in a cloud of gloom. They talked quietly and rarely laughed which was very unlike Maya's father, who had a booming voice and an even more resounding laugh. Her daughter was getting married into a very silent family and for some odd reason the thought saddened her.

Janaki had a strange sense of foreboding, a feeling that there was something amiss when she saw Kunal. She just could not lay her finger on it, could not comprehend exactly what it was that made her feel this way. The terrible sensation of something vaguely unpleasant lingered in her mind and continued to prey on her mind for the next few hours.

Maybe, Kunal's mother's death had left a lasting mark on both of them; maybe they were always this quiet, or *God forbid,* maybe, something was really wrong with the *boy!*

She allowed Kunal and Maya to go to the coffee house with an uneasy feeling. Later on, she attributed this uneasiness to simply a mother's worry for her daughter.

Maya's father, on the other hand, was his usual exuberant self. He found his wife's reaction to the *boy* completely unfounded and simply *overemotional.*

"Let the youngsters talk to each other, ji"!

"Let the boy and girl have a chance to ask some questions from each other. Don't be shy, beti."

"After all, it is their decision, ji"!

"He seems like a nice boy, haanji. Excellent, excellent. Excellent boy ji"

The driver was called and Kunal and Maya were dropped off to the nearby coffee house at a shopping plaza which (like any other place in New Delhi) was crowded to the point of bursting at its seams. After a few minutes of waiting in line, they were seated at the table.

"You know that I am still mad at you Mr. Kunal."

"Pray tell me, why?"

"Why did you cut me off completely? Why did you not let me know what was going on? You seemed to change a lot ever since you went to Mumbai when your mother fell sick in the second year. You refused to talk to me, and I tried so hard to get through to you," she ranted on without so much as drawing a breath.

"I know, and I am sorry for behaving that way."

"What do you mean? How can you say you are sorry? Ever since you came back from Mumbai, you were so distant, unapproachable and

hideous. I tried to talk to you and it just felt like I was banging my head against a brick wall."

"You must understand, my mother had been sick for a long time. She kept getting worse every time I visited her. She died in our last year of college. It was not easy for me to go through that. I was very close to her. Losing her was the biggest shock in my life. I was truly shaken up, but I am here now, aren't I?"

He smiled looking unblinking into her eyes, drowning in them and unable to peel his gaze away from them during the entire evening.

Their brief chat went on for two hours. Her old Kunal seemed to be back, with good looks, great sense of humor and a smile that lit up his eyes.

The fact that they were together again, that she did not have to go through the circus of meeting any more *boys and* that they were going to be married soon, brought endless happiness to her.

I am happy, she thought. "I have so much more happiness than heaven should ever allow," Maya remembered thinking selfishly.

CHAPTER ELEVEN

TILL DEATH DO US PART . . . 1988

The wedding was an exuberant affair, as befitted any Indian wedding. There were a million things to be taken care of and *there was shopping to be done!!*

There was ceaseless activity around the house, enough to tire even the strongest of all humans. In the midst of it all, her mother was the rock that held everything together, ordering everyone around, making lists, making plans and then cancelling them to make new plans, planning shopping trips*, in short,* getting overwhelmingly stressed and yet *enjoying every bit of it!*

Choosing her wedding dress, her jewelry and arranging the wedding ceremony, appeared to be all that her had mother lived for thus far in her life. She went on in a crazed manner, fixing this and that, constantly buying things for the house.

"*Clothes- oh my goodness- so many clothes*" had to be bought for Maya and everyone else for all the occasions that were planned for the wedding celebrations, gifts for the guests, the decorations, stressing over the menu for the food, crossing off some items from her long list and then adding many more.

In between this hot and hectic chaos, she would occasionally find a moment to sit with Maya and hug her and mourn the fact that she was going to leave her house forever, tearing up to let her know that she was going to miss her and that she loved her so very much.

Watching her mother was funny and sad at the same time: it reminded her of a spinning top that she used to play with when she was little. The constant whirring motion of the top mimicked the current state of her mother, spinning around its own axis until it suddenly slowed down and wobbled for a few turns and tipped over itself. Just like the top, her mother was an object in constant motion all day until fatigue overtook her. Exhausted to her core, every night she fell into a deep sleep as soon as she laid her head on the pillow.

There were times when Maya went and hid herself in her room. Looking out through the window, she nostalgically surveyed her backyard which was small but full of memories for her. The neatly maintained kitchen garden, the three orange trees and two lychee trees laden with fruit, surrounded by a patch of green chilies and tomatoes that were the "most delicious in the whole state" (*according to her father!*). The sunlight that filtered through the windows, the little portion of sky that she could see beyond the neighbor's unsightly fence, the birds chirping around and landing on to the clothesline, on which everyone's clothes, *including underwear,* unabashedly hanging to dry, almost made her choke with emotion. She was going to miss all this, her home where she was born and raised.

Soon, these sights would be gone and become a distant memory.

It was hard to believe that she would have to leave her home, the brick red duplex that her parents had recently renovated. She had been living in the Girls' Hostel at the campus for the last three years when she left for college at DCA. She had savored the luxury of coming home for the holidays or for weekends if the Girls' Hostel life started getting on her nerves.

Now, she was leaving this house forever, a rather sad prospect, notwithstanding the pomp and circumstance surrounding it.

For an Indian bride, her wedding is fraught with a multitude of anxious moments. Indian marriage is not only a union of a man and a woman; rather it is a marriage between two families.

The main character at the center of the show is the *mother-in-law*—the groom's mother. A son's wedding is the ultimate moment of glory for her. She has been waiting for this all her life, consciously or subconsciously. All the taunts that had been inflicted on her by her own mother-in-law, all her misgivings that had laid repressed and dormant in her memory for a whole generation suddenly turn green.

It is her turn now.

Life has come around a full circle and now is the time that *fate* has given her to exert her dominance. She is anxious to lay down the law and always have the upper hand in the relationship between her and the future daughter in law.

Meanwhile, the fathers in law chuckle at the pettiness of it all. The elders of the house sit back and reflect upon the progression of life and derive pride from witnessing the expansion of the clan. They are the ones who shower blessings with benevolent words that are benign and free of any suppressed angst.

Maya's friends were calling her with advice, about how it is important to stay in charge when dealing with the *mil, or sil, (sister n law),* how they were dealing with the tyrannical *in laws situation* at their end. When she interrupted their speech to tell them that Kunal's mother was deceased and she had no *sil* either, they would fall silent for a moment followed by, *"You are so lucky, Maya! How did you manage that?"*

Amid all this hoopla, Maya tried to fight back the waves of nausea brought on by sheer anxiety. The prospect of moving to unfamiliar surroundings, the immense heat of the month of June when the wedding was destined to be held *(as was ordained by the family priest),* the trips to the jeweler and the shopping centers, meetings with the photographer and the videographer, waiting in lines at the passport office and the immigration office at the US Consulate to get her visa to come to United States-all this was taking a toll on her. She was shriveling into a tiny bundle of nerves.

God only knew how she was going to look radiant and sublime on her wedding day!

Kunal was planning to move to Albany, a suburban city also the capital of the state of New York. His aunt (mother's sister) had sponsored his green card a few years ago and it had just come through. Already, he had a job offer to work as a designer at a very small, almost unknown architectural firm. The money was not much, the workload was substantial, but it was a start. It was definitely a foot in the door, and he wanted to work hard towards the goal of opening his own firm, one day.

In spite of the nervousness plaguing her, she was looking forward to starting a new chapter in her life. She was keenly awaiting an end to the wedding preparations and wished that she could fast forward to her wedding day.

They were so compatible, she thought happily. She imagined working together on joint projects, as architecture was their common passion, the places that they would travel to, the friends they would meet, the small modern house that they would decorate; all this was very exciting.

Kunal, her soon to be husband, was extremely loving, and teased her constantly about their upcoming honeymoon.

Her wedding day was a blur in her mind. She remembered thinking that there should be a simpler way for two people to get married. She had to wear the heavily embroidered wedding *lehnga,* which weighed her slight figure down. She had to wear jewelry which pinched her, her shoes were high heeled and threatened an embarrassing fall any moment. It was hot in the banquet hall filled with hundreds of people, as if the whole town had been invited for this occasion. Then came the wait for the appropriate *mahurat* which was at 2 am. This was determined by the respected priest, for it enabled the correct alignment of the stars to hold the seven circles around the fire which made the marriage sacred not only in the eyes of humans but was also blessed by the gods themselves.

The ceremony lasted forever. Not much of it was understandable, as the entire Hindu wedding ceremony is conducted in *Sanskrit*, a very difficult and complex language. There were a million traditions to be followed, about a hundred pictures to be taken, a video to be made and at the end of what seemed like 8 hours it was over.

She was officially *Mrs. Maya Sinha* now.

CHAPTER TWELVE

LOOKING FOR . . .
AMERICA 1988

Life started for Kunal and Maya really well. It was typical in many ways. There was the usual excitement of a newlywed immigrant couple, trying to settle in the United States of America.

They were not their parents' children anymore. All of a sudden, they had become full grown adults! They were now the masters of their own destiny. No tradition had to be followed and no elders had to be consulted for each major decision; they could do whatever they pleased. They could wear what they wanted, sleep in if they wanted, eat what they wanted, say what they wanted and there was no one to point a finger at them. It was a very liberating feeling for them.

They were strangers in a strange country, and they felt like pioneers forging a new life onto a new land.

It was as if a blank canvas had been offered to them and they could splash any colors that they liked. There were no rules, they could do whatever suited their fancy.

There was stuff to be bought every day. New beds and furniture and linens and towels and kitchen utensils; it gave Maya immense pleasure to rip the packaging off all the new things they brought into their apartment every day.

This wave of excitement lasted a month.

Soon, the mundane things and routines that make up *"LIFE"* started creeping into their youthful existence: the cooking and cleaning and the paying of the bills.

These were however overshadowed by the exceptional treasure that they shared: their love.

Kunal was sure that their love was unparalleled and unique. He could not imagine that anyone else in the entire history of creation had known love such as theirs. It was a heady feeling to wake up next to Maya every day.

Each day spent together was marked with a unique beauty and each sunset watched together had a soft romantic sheen to it. He could live his entire life like that wrapped up in her beauty, listening to her talk, watch her laugh and lose himself in the deep kisses that were offered to him very generously.

His office was close to the apartment, the drive took him barely fifteen minutes. She started her day with a quick breakfast for him and lazed around, watched tv for an obnoxious duration of time. She also was very fond of cooking and was trying to get more adept at Indian cooking by watching the FOOD channel!

Her *choo-choo* train of happiness got a minor jolt when she realized that after accounting for all the taxes and monthly expenses, there was barely 200 dollars left over. There was not too much that could be done with that! She was not used to worrying about bills or money when she lived in her father's house. Her parents were not rich, but they were not poor either. She realized that she will have to start budgeting (*what an ugly word*).

In other words, she will have to shop less and save more, or she had to get a *job*.

Kunal and Maya had very few friends. Akshay, Kunal's best friend who was also from Mumbai, was the only person that they knew. He lived in an apartment nearby and worked for the same architectural firm as Kunal's. Their projects were mainly from small businesses and included small jobs such as office buildings and small residential projects.

Akshay's wife, Devyani, was working at a clothing store at the mall. Just like Kunal and Maya, they were recently married. Akshay was Kunal's friend from high school days and he finished his training in architecture from DAC (Delhi Architectural College). He was also Kunal's constant drinking buddy while in college, Maya remembered bitterly, holding Akshay responsible for Kunal's *alcoholic* period.

Akshay and Kunal had discussed moving to US when they were in college. They had spent many hours familiarizing and educating themselves regarding immigration requirements. Kunal's aunt had sponsored him for a green card and it was easy for him to come to America.

Akshay did not have anyone to sponsor him: he decided to marry his way into America. Devyani was born and raised in US and her father knew Akshay's father from childhood. As their children got older, they decided to turn their friendship into a matrimonial alliance.

Devyani had met Akshay on her trips to India and had always liked him. She had dated multiple guys in Delaware, where she was born and raised. Somehow, she had not found anyone that she could consider spending her life with. When her parents suggested that she should marry Akshay, she was happy. She was also relieved that she could now quit the dating scene, *(she had had enough first dates)* and finally settle down and have babies.

Akshay and Kunal met up almost every weekend and soon the wives became good friends as well. Soon enough, Maya wanted to get a job for extra money. The lack of money was starting to bother her. She had sent out applications for jobs at the nearby architectural firms, but her efforts had not yielded any response.

She would have to get some more training in architectural design, get some experience as an apprentice and clear a qualifying exam, before she would have a shot at a decent job.

Kunal and Akshay were smart as they had started their job search while they were still in college. They had sent their applications to multiple headhunter companies and were lucky to have an offer from three companies. After much deliberation, they decided to accept offers from the same company. It would be of immense help to stick together in the new country, where they had no close family members to speak of. Their compensation was not much, but they were happy to get a break this early in their career.

The lack of money had started to weigh on Maya. She wanted a job, any job and started to look for one obsessively. For any meaningful job, driving was absolutely essential. Public transportation, which was easily available in India, was nonexistent in her town. Everyone in US, young or old, man or woman, *drove.*

She needed a driving license, and for that she would absolutely have to take the *hateful* driving test. It entailed learning to drive a car and that was a formidable task for her. She had never driven a car in India. She had *learnt,* but she was always driven to places that she needed to go. Her dad, her cousins, her friends would drive her, or if it was absolutely urgent, she would take a cab.

In America, everyone drove on the *opposite* side of the road. That was the first challenge- to forget all she knew about driving in India and to start completely from scratch. With a loathsome heart she started to memorize the traffic rules and regulations and after a nerve-racking month of practicing, she was able to pass her driving test.

A nearby Dunkin Donuts needed a *cashier* and she applied for the job. It would barely pay her the minimum wage: a mere *eight dollars an hour.* But it was *money,* something that was in real short supply for Maya and Kunal at the time.

She felt very out of place in the first few days. Her accent and dark Indian features attracted many questions from the customers. Some questions were amusing and made her laugh inwardly. It was amazing to learn how little the American people knew about India, how commonly they confused India with Pakistan, who in reality were sworn enemies. Arranged marriage was another question which featured in the questions on a regular basis and try as much as she might, she could never explain it enough. All her answers in that regard were met with a quizzical smile.

She worked as many hours as she could manage. All her expensive Indian clothes were of no use to her as she could not wear those to work on a daily basis. She had to wear a uniform and actually she did not mind it at all.

Somewhere along the way, she realized that she was enjoying her independence and her new lifestyle of being in the employed workforce. She enjoyed her job even though it was only a *menial job (as her father would say)* as a cashier.

She was getting used to having a little extra money and was able to buy some of the luxuries that she had denied herself such as make up, shoes, nail appointments, occasionally a bottle of perfume. She spoke to Devyani on a regular basis and was very thankful for her friendship.

Devyani was the best shopping companion any person could ever hope for. With Devyani's ample help Maya was able to figure out where to buy trendy clothes on the cheap, learn about fashion and also learn about which bars and restaurants to go to, to have a good time.

With Kunal's help, she found out about the required courses for her to have a shot at a real job in the architectural field and Maya enrolled herself for night classes. Her weekdays were spent at Dunkin Donuts, nights were spent taking classes and her weekends were spent studying and preparing for the exams.

She became busy, although stressed, had more money as compared to before and was finally living the *American Dream!*

Even though she was busy, she felt terribly homesick at times. She was thankful for the hours spent at work, when she did not have the chance to dwell on how strange it was to live in a new country, so far away from her doting parents. Initially, the food did not taste good to her, especially the Indian food in Indian restaurants.

She started to cook herself and still could not get the food to taste the same as she remembered it from her childhood. She wanted to figure out what it was that made the food taste different; she used the same ingredients, the same spices as her mother used back home. If only she could pinpoint what it was, find out and fix the one reason why it was so hard to duplicate the flavors and the tastes that she had grown up with!

It was very frustrating for her and she felt that she ate the food but did not really relish it. All Indian food, homemade or otherwise, tasted bland and foreign. The terrible homesickness and the foreignness of a new culture made her sick to her stomach and often left her struggling to fit in.

Additionally, a new nagging fear had started to take a hold on her, which sometimes drove her to tears. She wondered if and when she would ever see her parents again. Every phone call from her parents worried her, she feared for their health and well-being and entreated them to take good care of themselves.

She was not going to be able to visit them for a long time.

Air tickets to India were not *cheap*.

CHAPTER THIRTEEN

WRAPPED AROUND
YOUR FINGER - 1994

Luck was finally turning for Kunal. His boss was becoming more appreciative of his work and considered him his righthand man. He was getting more projects and money was starting to come in.

His job was becoming more enjoyable and it was exhilarating to see his designs get transformed into real buildings, even though these were not the skyscrapers that he had imagined building all his adult years. In reality, these were small office buildings, glorified halls divided by cabin dividers into cubicles, unimaginative, routine and mundane work; but at least he was getting paid to build these!

His first independent project was an indoor garage for a small office. His compensation money was in the form of a bonus in addition to his salary. It was a *staggering* $ 7000, and it meant a better car for them and a long overdue vacation.

Apart from work, his thoughts were mainly to keep Maya happy. During their trips to the mall he saw her eyes light up briefly when she saw something in the display window followed by a sigh when she found out how much it cost. It made him wince inwardly when he saw how quickly the pleasure vanished from her face.

He loved to buy gifts for her. Even though they were inexpensive, he knew that she cherished them. She made it a point to use them to make him happy. The silk scarf that was her favorite shade of pink *(bought in a sale at the drugstore when he went to buy shaving supplies for himself, later on he learnt it was pure polyester!)* the perfume which she used every day, the keychain with the likeness of lord Ganesha bought from the Indian store, she used all of these with pride and a fondness so true that it was touching.

With the bonus money, he wanted to lease a new car for Maya. It would be a nice surprise gift for her and …he was really excited about this…they will visit New York, the city of their dreams! Just to be at the top floor of the Empire State Building would be truly mind blowing!

Maya would especially enjoy the visit; she had mentioned many times that they should take a trip to the Big Apple.

He was saving the experience for their upcoming anniversary. He was happy and her smile made him happier and his day even brighter. His life began and ended with thoughts of her. She was the center of his universe. He could happily spend the rest of his life basking in the warmth of her playful gaze, her gentle words and heartfelt laughter.

He fell into a reverie, thinking of the time they met, of how unsure he was of Maya's love in the beginning. If he knew then how she felt about him, he would have proposed sooner.

If only he had known *sooner* that she loved him enough to marry him!

If only he had known *sooner* that living with her would be so easy!

All that time spent thinking and hesitating was time *lost forever.*

Everything could have been so different. She would even have accepted his mother, even with the ugliness of her disease, if she were alive.

"If she were alive!"

The thought of his mother made him shiver inside and he wiped a small droplet of sweat that was beginning to form on his forehead.

"But again, who really knows?" he thought as his forehead knotted into a question.

Anyways, today he was happy. He was driving to the car dealership. She would love the midnight blue color sedan he had chosen for her. He had called ahead and had the salesman at the dealership reserve the car.

Navy blue was her favorite color, he thought fondly.

The trip to New York should be exciting as well. After all it was the greatest city in the whole world: undoubtedly an architectural wonder. He could visualize her eyes filling with delight which only happened when her heart was happy.

He had already planned out the trip. In addition to doing all the touristy things, the Empire State Building, the Statue of Liberty, Times Square, he was going to surprise her with a Broadway show.

CHAPTER FOURTEEN

INTO THE MADDING CROWD . . . 1995

New York was absolutely breathtaking. When Maya saw the skyline of the city in the distance, she could feel the excitement building in her heart. The crowded streets reminded her of her parental home in New Delhi.

Unlike their quiet suburban town near Albany, this city was teeming with people. She realized how much she had missed seeing crowds and crowds of *people*. In New York there were hundreds of people walking at the same time. In her town, she barely saw anyone on the street. She could hardly catch a glimpse of her own neighbors as they drove by her faceless and hidden in their cars.

In New York, the streets here were alive with a life of their own, as compared to the desolate little town that they lived in.

It was a city built to an unfathomable scale. The enormous cityscape, the subway system, the gigantic billboards in Times Square, everything about the city made her seem small and insignificant. There was a humming noise, a vibration that was ever present in the city. It was alive and it possessed a pulse of its own that she could feel resonating within herself.

As she stood on the side of the busy streets and breathed in the city, a little polluted and dirty, *just like New Delhi,* she felt herself being engulfed, becoming a part of the greatest city in the world.

The yellow cabs were everywhere. The fashionably dressed women strutting in high heels walked past her purposefully to destinations that were infinitely important. There were young men dressed in suits, walking at a breakneck pace. It seemed as if everyone who lived here had somewhere important to go to, as if time was running out for them at a more rapid pace than they could keep up with.

Maya felt diminutive as compared to the sheer magnitude of the surroundings around her. She stepped uncertainly, unsure, second guessing herself at every avenue, awestruck by the sheer concrete beauty of the city and painfully aware of her own insignificance and the almost cruel indifference of people walking around her.

All this was in sharp contrast to what she was accustomed to in her suburban neighborhood. All of a sudden, she did not feel like an immigrant who was different due to her appearance. In this sea of people from all walks of life and all possible nationalities, she was not *peculiar* anymore.

Even though she was reduced to mere blur due to the gigantic buildings around her, yet Maya started to feel free, liberated and suddenly had a sense of belonging for the first time in this brand-new country. America had been a strange land to her so far.

Now she felt as if this was her *home!*

She could lose herself in this crowd and finally start to exist, and be, rather than always being the odd one out. In her town she was forever explaining her origin, her attire and her culture to people who heard her, without understanding her. She did not get any curious looks here, in New York and that was a welcome change for her.

She told Kunal about how she felt safe and secure in this huge crowd and he looked at her quizzically, smiling at her and nodding oddly. His face wore an expression of someone trying to understand a strange concept, still unsure of what she really meant, yet agreeing with her patronizingly.

CHAPTER FIFTEEN

DESIRE NOT, WANT NOT . . . 1995

After returning from the trip to New York, her tiny suburban neighborhood seemed even smaller. Her apartment and her way of life seemed diminutive in comparison to what she had seen in her brief visit to the big city.

For a few days the impression of living a shrunken version of life as compared to New York hung like a cloud over her head. She did not want to keep living in such a small lifeless neighborhood anymore. She wished that she was one of the smartly clad New York women, hurrying about the street, going somewhere. Their little suburban town was so small. Even her lifestyle, her clothes, her life seemed even more insignificant as compared to before.

She wanted more, *so much more!*

She wanted to travel *more,* shop more, meet *more* people and have *more* money. Her life seemed *small* and restrictive. Her low paying job hardly seemed to be worthwhile. She found herself highly dissatisfied with the way things were and a strange emptiness had come over her.

Maya wondered if Kunal felt the same way, or if he could perceive this change in her outlook. A discontented spirit had made a home in her soul, and she could feel herself getting angry and frustrated with every little thing.

She had noticed his strange moods lately. There were times when he seemed to be lost in space and his face acquired the expression of brooding thoughtfulness. During those long silences, he stared at nothing in particular and on some occasions, she had to physically shake him out of his trance. These moments were usually brought on by any talk pertaining to his mother.

Slowly, Maya learnt to avoid that topic as it was obviously, a painful issue for Kunal.

Luckily, there was no silence long enough for him to ignore her charms, especially when she was in a good mood. It was great that they were both young and in love and self-confessed architectural geeks.

Many of their discussions would start from Frank Lloyd Wright, touch upon the giants of French architecture and end with intense lovemaking.

However, ever since their visit to New York, Kunal's jokes were not as funny anymore and did not make Maya laugh. His smiling eyes did not warm up her soul like they used to.

She was embarrassed to admit even to herself, that Kunal was not her entire life anymore. He was not the *be all and end all of her life,* as he used to be! For the last six years that she had known him, he had surfaced in every conscious thought that she had, and now he had definitely become a lot less significant. She felt foolish but she was sure that a change was coming over her and it was making her see everything in a different light including Kunal.

"Did the visit to New York do that?" she wondered. *"Do I see him differently now, just because I have been to a different city for 5 days? How truly shallow am I?"*

"Maybe, we are not meant to be soul mates. Maybe, there is someone else for each of us! It is a big wide world out there. Who really knows?"

These thoughts were very strange for Maya. She felt oddly irreverent and immoral just for thinking them. For someone who had never ventured out of her sheltered life in India, a husband is a permanent figure of respect, next only to Almighty God. Now, she could feel the fabric of her moral accoutrement slowly ripping at the seams, making her a feel a little depraved with every tear.

She could not understand this change in herself.

She wondered if she would soon go back to being who she was. It was better and less complicated that way.

"Really, how could a visit to a city change her?"

"Or maybe, it is me…"

CHAPTER SIXTEEN

BABY, OH BABY . . . 1995

Kunal was very happy at this stage in life.

He had found a more comfortable condominium and was looking forward to moving into a spacious place to live in as compared to their tiny apartment. All his friends were having babies and starting a family was the most important thought on his mind as well.

His father wanted a grandchild and had started hinting at it, partly jokingly.

Kunal had been fixated on his career so far. He had successfully progressed in his professional life due to his hard work and relentless effort.

Maya and Kunal had made great friends among their community and weekends were spent socializing, hosting and attending parties, concerts and taking small trips whenever the work schedule allowed.

Now, the next item on his agenda was *having a baby*.

His friends' jokes and snide remarks had started to sting a little and make a home in his brain.

Additionally, his relatives were starting to drop not so subtle hints.

"Should you be seeing a doctor and finding out what is wrong? After all, it has been four years since your marriage; even our neighbors are starting to ask questions!!"

The discussion about planning to have child was also the source of their first major fight as a married couple.

Maya felt that she still needed time.

She felt that she was still so new to this country.

She was still unsure whether she was ready to be a mother yet.

These were the same reasons that she brought up repeatedly, each time the *baby discussion* came up.

What she could not admit to Kunal was that *finally she was independent. She was making her own money, little though it was, she was starting to like it!*

Having a baby now would put a damper on her newly found life, classes, and her architectural diploma that she was working day and night for.

He was totally unaware of her real reasons for delaying the baby, as she could not tell him that. She would be considered a selfish and unmotherly woman for harboring these thoughts.

It was much easier to just fight and walk away in tears!

"By God, Maya, I love you dearly, but this is getting to be annoying. Would you just stay and talk to me for two minutes before *you walk out on me again?"*

She would not have any further discussion about it.

Kunal was becoming more and more persistent about having a baby. Maya's architectural school diploma was still a distant dream. She knew that she could not ward him off much longer.

He was getting increasingly outraged about her lack of interest in having a baby with every discussion.

Soon, these discussions turned into heated arguments that ended with shouting matches and angry epithets.

She felt more and more unwilling to conceive a baby in the middle of all such mental turmoil. She wanted to be completely sure before she would consider bringing a child into this world.

As this went on, Maya's night classes seemed to get longer. She started finding excuses for not coming home right away. Once in a while, she started staying over at a friend's apartment to finish her assignments.

Kunal's disdain and anger directed at her drained all her ambition. She lost the ability to do her studying in the midst of all the negativity emanating from him. Earlier, she used to rush home right after class, as she wanted to be home for having dinner with him.

Now, the constant fighting made her want to stay back longer.

One night, at the end of class, she was once again delaying going home. She aimlessly walked along the street trying to clear her mind before heading home. Almost absentmindedly, she stepped into an adjoining Starbucks.

It felt strangely exhilarating, to be at a coffee shop when she should actually have been rushing home, preparing dinner!

It felt like cutting class back in high school!

She deliberately sat down, ordered herself a doughnut and enjoyed her coffee, sipping slowly. The aroma filled her with a strange sense of freedom, almost sinful. With each passing minute, rushing home to have dinner with Kunal became more and more irrelevant. She stayed until she was done with her assignment and then drove home. By the time she got home it was 11:30 pm.

Maya had never returned home this late!

It was during one of her trips to the coffee shop that she became aware of *him*.

She always sat in the corner furthest from the door, and *he* always sat at the table right across from her. There was a passing smile and a nod in the beginning and then that changed to a *hello* with a smile.

By the fourth meeting, she was wearing her best outfit, and she caught herself smoothing her hair and wishing for lip gloss in her purse. She was embarrassed to admit to herself that she was attracted to *him*.

"Would you mind very much if I join you?" *he* said *(on their fifth meeting)*.

He was employed by one of the computer companies and was taking a graphic design course, in her class, *he* told her.

Of course, she knew that. She had seen *him* in class many times!

"I see you working on assignments after every class," *he* said.

"Yes. I find it easier to finish them right after class. Once I reach home, I procrastinate," she involuntarily smiled at *him*.

"Oh, Good! Then, we can work on it together and finish it in half the time! I hope you don't mind?"

After that they sat together after class over a cup of coffee and she started looking forward to seeing *him*. They discussed the common assignments and worked on them together. She was slowly starting to notice *his* eyes behind the thick rimmed glasses, *his* day-old stubble, *his* tired wrinkled shirt collar at the end of a long day at work.

She was starting to get comfortable addressing *him* by his first name (Anthony). *He* was able to pronounce her name perfectly, which was a welcome change for someone not familiar with Indian names!

He was not particularly handsome to look at. He was a little heavy set, almost balding at his forehead, his complexion was pure white, and his face was marked by splotches of red discoloration. Yet, she was attracted to him.

"It is only *companionship*," she rationalized to herself. "It is only *cerebral*."

Every time they spoke to each other, their eyes locked wordlessly for a few seconds.

Eventually, she found that she was overwhelmingly attracted to him.

It was imperative that she should smell his cologne and touch the dark spot on his neck that peeked from underneath his shirt collar. His slightly imperfect nose, prominent Adam's apple, his watch, all these caught her fancy. There was tremendous electricity that surrounded him.

And she did not even think that he was good looking!

"*I am obviously glorifying him, just like a teenager, with a crush,*" justified Maya.

Many weeks of contemplation, doubt, blushing at her thoughts and strict self criticism passed by. Maya thought about *him* all the time.

All this was very troublesome. She constantly felt a vice around her head, crushing her skull with intolerable pressure all the time, so much so, that at times, she felt that her head would burst from the ongoing mental turmoil.

Needless to say, her mental turbulence was casting a shadow on her married life.

She did not plan on acting on any of her thoughts. Kunal was the only man she had ever known and honestly, she did not want to do anything to ruin her marriage. *Anthony* was a closely guarded guilty secret that she planned on keeping locked away in her mind.

In spite of her best efforts, however, she thought about *him* constantly, obsessively. She felt her terrible fixation feeding on her mind and slowly metamorphosing into a monster that she wanted to be liberated from.

She was really *not* looking for any nonsensical complication at this juncture of her life.

"Are you not willingly encouraging this demon with your fancy and imagination?" her conscience (or what was left of it) accused her angrily all the time.

Her internal conversation with her conscience was getting increasingly loud and deafening.

CHAPTER SEVENTEEN

THE FLESH
INDEED IS . . . WEAK 1996

"I should stop seeing him altogether!"
Or
"I should sleep with him once and that will take care of it."

The latter thought was now appearing to be a solution, ridiculous though it might be.

Maya was caught in a situation that she had never found herself in before. Her only sexual experience had been with Kunal and lately that had become more of a chore than a joy. She was not really looking to experiment with promiscuity or leaving the safe perimeter of her marriage.

Yet, she was strangely powerless when she was in Anthony's presence.

She did not even cringe as he placed his hand on her back as they entered the coffee shop. She also had started to get used to his arm across her shoulders for brief moments. She was getting comfortable with him around her and this surprised and worried her at the same time.

She questioned her morality constantly. She understood that she was not capable of thinking through the hazy cloud that overpowered her judgment. Her conscience provided her with so many sharp criticisms of her that she stopped listening to it. Her thoughts were getting blurred, slowly her mind grew complacent and eventually she quit analyzing the situation, *altogether*.

CHAPTER EIGHTEEN

LISTEN TO YOUR HEART??
1996

Maya's heart, on the other hand, told her clearly, that she should definitely *not* stop seeing *him*. Sinful, though it may be, her clandestine *affair* made her feel so full of life that she was definitely not going to end it.

Not just yet!

Yet, she desired a culmination to this scenario. A part of her mind was curious to know where this could lead to. Maybe, that was why she did not resist when *he* caught her hand one day and was almost relieved when *he* pulled her close to kiss her.

Lately, she had stopped looking herself in the mirror. It was very foreign to her, to be immoral. She could not believe that she was now an *adulteress*. She was raised to be a typical Indian wife, devoted to her husband and her family.

Now, she was not comfortable in her own skin anymore. She was constantly troubled by her guilt.

She was *not* going to prolong this errant sojourn; she was *definitely* going to end it.

Soon.

There was no one that she could talk to about this either. All her friends were such perfect wives and were so perfectly devoted to their families that she could not even consider discussing it with them. She would instantly be labeled as a harlot and an *easy* woman.

There would be no one who would understand her. They would instantly take sides. They would pass judgement: she would be singled out as the wrongdoer and Kunal would be the wronged spouse.

And they would be right...

Her covert meetings with *Tony*, were becoming more and more passionate. Soon the cups of coffee transformed into dinner and class assignments and meetings started extending into the daytime hours.

A trip to San Francisco was a mandatory requirement for the course; for the study of architecture of the unique cityscape of the iconic city. Their assignment was to research and compile a presentation on the structural details of the Golden Gate Bridge.

The entire class of twenty-five students flew along with their instructor to San Francisco. She was eagerly anticipating the day of their flight. She felt like a schoolgirl about to go on a much-awaited field trip. Her heart hummed with a loud throb of excitement throughout the flight.

Their hotel rooms were on the same floor. They were trying to be extremely discreet about their liaison, even though, none of the other students really seemed to care. They were mostly comprised of tired adults who had poor paying day jobs. They wanted to get the diploma so that they could have better jobs and start making more money, *exactly the reason that she had joined this course!*

After a full day of listening to the boring talk from their course leader and walking all day they in the city, the whole group met for an early dinner at a Chinese restaurant at the Ghirardelli Square. It was a perfect evening with a mild ocean breeze and a sound of ocean waves in the distance. *They* could barely keep their eyes away from each other.

The group split up after dinner and he offered to walk her to the hotel room.

It was still early, and she suggested a walk along the beach. The heady ocean breeze, the sand which had cooled a little, the waves roaring constantly, and the wine that *(she had started drinking now, something she did not do in Kunal's presence)* she had guzzled rather excessively during dinner seemed to dull her senses.

Thick clouds traveled along the breeze and enveloped the shiny moon and the darkness around them was almost complete.

His hand lingered on hers and they stopped talking. He kissed her on the lips, slowly, lazily. In the strange city there was no fear of being found out and that knowledge alone was an aphrodisiac by itself.

It had started to drizzle now, and they were still kissing. The thunder and lightning made them hurry towards the hotel. *He* followed her into her room and laughed at the amount of sand they had dragged into the room on their shoes.

She had to get out of the wet, clothes and really needed a shower. As she showered and changed, her brain was trying to think but she was too excited to formulate any coherent thoughts. *He* called room service and ordered a bottle of champagne.

He poured her a glass and as she sipped it, licked her lips.

"Hmmm, tastes much better from your lips."

Slowly, the champagne was gone, and so were her inhibitions. He was trailing kisses on her neck. He lifted her nightshirt over her.

The rest of the night was a dim memory covered with layers of guilt. She remembered waking up in shame and disgust, angry at her own reflection in the bathroom mirror. She quickly got dressed and left the room.

She went to the lounge and gulped down two cups of coffee.

It was then that she knew that it was over.

Literally.

She told *him* the next morning that she was never going to see *him* again. *He* was shocked and started to say something to make her change her mind but the stony resolve in her eye stopped him and *he* left her room.

This was definitely the turning point in her life.

She felt as if she had climbed on top of a giant mountain and was all alone atop the ghastly emptiness of a deep dark valley below, barely able to breathe the cold thin air. No matter how hard and deep she inhaled, she was left gasping.

She felt like a criminal who had committed the perfect crime, leaving no proof whatsoever and was never going to get caught. The punishment of the crime was only going to be a slow, gradual simmer in lifelong guilt.

She was the one who had tainted the sanctity of her marriage.

She was *dirty, evil and immoral*, a voice kept on reminding her, reproachfully; she had shamed herself, what she had done was forbidden and treacherous and defied all the values that had been instilled into her. She was disappointed at the sordid mess she found herself in. She could feel her *soul* dying within her.

Her inner self shook an accusing finger at her and warned her of *the effects of bad karma.*

There will be a price to be paid for this!
The universe will demand a payback!

CHAPTER NINETEEN

I AM HOME NOW . . . 1997

After her return from San Francisco, Maya was busy with her exams and her job applications. It was as if she was back in school again. Once again, the late hours of studying were required. She was heading home every night right after her job ended to cram up as much as possible.

She was free of guilt as she was living the life of a *pure and moral* wife. She felt inwardly relieved and her body and mind were in perfect harmony. She was able to focus; her curriculum was manageable; she was home every night; the sight of Kunal did not irritate her anymore, they were once again discussing plans for a family: everything seemed to move along fluidly, with a positive energy.

She passed her exam with flying colors. After she finished her course, she was able to land a job in a government owned company. The salary was nowhere close to Kunal's, but her hours were easier.

She was happy now. Her home life was free of obstacles. Kunal was able to see a major change in Maya as they started planning for a child. At this point, *she* wanted to have a baby, and he was thrilled to know that.

Their love for each other, which had been missing for the last two years, came back into their lives. Once again, to every discerning eye, they were a perfect couple: good looking, in step with the times, with a cool condominium furnished in a very modern, contemporary vibe. They were in good health, daily treadmill and weekly gym routine was the one thing they never missed.

They remembered each other's birthdays. Gourmet dinners were planned for their frequent *date nights*. Their gifts to each other were meaningful, even lavish.

They were not hurting financially, and the future spread in front of them as a lush inviting landscape.

Their friends were envious of the perfect couple that they were!

CHAPTER TWENTY

PEA IN A POD . . . 1998

"*Why does the mind slow down when you are pregnant?*" Maya thought angrily.

She wished that all the scientists in the world could devote some time and figure this one out.

"*Just the imbalance of hormones,*" was what her obstetrician said.

That was just not an adequate enough explanation for Maya as she shook her head at some imaginary Einstein who had come up with this reason. According to her, the real reason was the diversion of blood flow away from the *intelligent* portions of the brain to the growing placenta and fetus and whatever it was in the brain that made her *hungry!*

As her pregnancy advanced, Maya became more sluggish and slept all the time. Her body was enlarging and her movements and thinking processes were getting slower! When her initial nausea abated, all she could think of was food, ice cream and doughnuts; and she was eating all of these items: *abundantly!*

She was in the last trimester of her pregnancy and at Kunal's insistence, she had taken the next six months off. She had applied for a sabbatical at work and spent most of her time ruminating philosophically.

Indian marriage, she thought, was a double-edged knife. It cut both ways. On one hand, it was a snug and warm security blanket which offered comfort, warmth and protection. It provided shelter from the world like a pleasant, secure refuge. It was a successful financial arrangement for two persons to pool their resources *(Kunal's money had been growing and had definitely made her life easier)* and raise a family, grow together as a unit and merge into the *(Indian)* society so easily.

"A married woman was sure to be invited everywhere. Take the husband out of the picture and women start demonizing you."

On the other hand, it was rather boring! It was lifelong, mandatory and binding in the society's eyes. It could easily become an unpleasant accord if the partners lacked connection and had different expectations from life. In that case, it could turn into a disastrous nightmare and taint two lives, much like rust eating into iron. It worked well only if the individuals involved were in perfect harmony and their stars were favorably aligned. It was like flipping a coin; there was a 50% likelihood of coming out victorious.

"It is no one's fault. You throw two well-meaning people into a house for a life sentence, someone is going to develop prison fever sometime!"

All the same, most of us *(married people)* sign up for it, drink to it, enjoy it, embrace it and celebrate it with song and dance; so much so that we want to relive and remember the day year after year after year.

"How many anniversary parties does it take to finally realize the monotony of the whole ordeal," she questioned herself warily.

"Ah," she thought reflecting over her life. *"Was I always such a cynic?"*

"Not really."

Maya could remember when love was the most important thing for her; it had mattered more than all material things, more than power, fame or anything. All her values, desires, ideas and hopes, if she could crystallize them all in one word, it would be *love*.

She had really not asked for much from life. What had always mattered to her was *simplicity, truth and love.* The simple days, the sunrises and the sunsets, the simple chirping of the birds, the spectacular display of nature when it became cloudy and stormed, the simple music that she liked, classical instrumental compositions on the sitar, occasional jazz renditions of Louis Armstrong and *(even at the risk of being cheesy)* Kenny G, the simple taste of foods that she grew up with, the simple ingredients that awoke her taste buds and nourished her just the same: these were the inexpensive joys that were sufficient to satisfy her for the expanse of her entire life.

In her mind, romance, needed to be pure and absolute to bring joy. There was no place for argument in an ideal relationship. In a perfect, loving, relationship, things should flow spontaneously, like the flow of a lazy river, at ease and in perfect harmony with all the elements of the universe.

She would desire nothing more from life if there was no conflict in daily life and she could have a purposeful existence. She really did not crave diamonds or gems. All she needed was peace and a conflict-free existence. Ideally, her entire life should be an expression of love, not a maze of questions that left you exhausted and looking for answers.

Kunal was her soul mate and her confidant, her co traveler in this journey of life. They had embarked on this voyage and made an eternal promise in the presence of God to be true to each other as they as she maneuvered the hurdles that came along their way.

In her mind her truancy with Anthony was a hurdle.

For a brief while, life had become truly magical. They were so much in sync that they would often be humming the same tune, he could read her deepest thoughts without her saying a single word and she could tell what he was going to order at a restaurant before he told the waiter.

They were completely coherent in body and soul, liking the same foods, listening to same music, reading the same authors. Days, and nights were just perfect. Many times, she would smell him on the pillow and be overcome with great affection for him. She could even feel his presence in the house even when he was gone.

She sighed when she realized how perfect her life was.

Sonu was born in their sixth year of marriage and Kunal was the proudest father that ever walked on the face of this earth.

Then, suddenly, just like a bolt of lightning, on Kunal's *thirty sixth* birthday, in the middle of his *supposedly* surprise birthday party hosted by Maya, things seemed to change forever.

CHAPTER
TWENTY ONE

HAPPY BIRTHDAY
TO YOU . . . 2004

Yes, it was a happy day, today.

Maya was excited and all her thoughts ran through her mind as if in the rhythm of a happy song. She had arranged a *"surprise"* birthday party for Kunal. Of course, like all husbands who have ever been thrown a surprise birthday party, he seemed to go along with the *surprise* part of it. She had invited about fifteen couples who were all going to be hiding in her house waiting to *surprise* Kunal when he returned home from work.

A cake was already on the cake table. All of the decorations were an attempt to create a *gothic cathedral theme*, an architectural style that Kunal could wax eloquent about for hours. Even the disposable cups had *Notre Dame* inscribed on them.

Maya wore a red dress, and her hair was pulled back and coiffed into a "*French chignon*".

She had also bought a very thoughtful gift for Kunal, a DVD collection of his favorite movies. Some of them were so old that it had taken her a long time to find in the store. This would be a party to remember; just for the special touches she had added to every little detail.

People showed up on time. Maya ran and checked herself in the mirror one final time and told herself that she looked just lovely!

The food was plentiful and delicious; the lamb chops had the right amount of char and the right amount of spice, the cocktails were flowing effortlessly, thanks to the two mixologists that she had hired instead of one; the music was mellow, and the mood was truly festive in a cool, understated sort of way.

All in all, it had the makings of the best surprise birthday party that a wife could have ever arranged for a husband!

She was genuinely excited to see the look on Kunal's face as he entered the house to a loud shout of "Happy Birthday" and the multiple hugs that followed. The night of frivolity and celebration had gone on till 2 in the morning, and as the last lingering couple left, she was smug in the knowledge that this had truly been an epic party.

It took two hours of clean up in the morning. Finally, her house had started to look like itself again.

She was sipping her morning cup of tea and she heard Kunal's footsteps as he climbed down the staircase. As he came to sit upon the couch next to her and she happily turned to look at him. Maya could immediately tell that he did not seem like his usual self. He had a brooding look about him, his hands jerked as if he was trying to wave away an invisible gnat, repeatedly.

All her questions to him were answered in a monosyllabic response. He did not look at her in the eye. He seemed to focus at a point slightly above her right shoulder. It reminded her vaguely of the time when he had disappeared from the college for three months, around the time of his mother's death. His eyes had the same vacant look that had filled his eyes then.

However, he also seemed to be mumbling something in a low tone. She could not understand what he was saying. This scared her to the point where she took him by the shoulders and shook him, shouting his name.

To Maya's surprise, Kunal screamed loudly as he shoved her away, powerfully enough to send her reeling into the furniture. Maya's forehead had small dots of blood appear that rapidly started streaming down her cheek.

Maya ran to her son's room and locked herself. Almost desperately, she reached for her phone and called Shabnam.

Of late, Shabnam and Maya were best friends.

Maya had met her at a friend's house and as they chatted, she found that they had a lot of common interests. Both of them were working women, fond of shopping and cooking and art movies. Their tastes were a little different from the rest of the Indian moms in their circle.

Shabnam was divorced. She knew that most women avoided associating with her. She was frequently left out of a lot of social gatherings and family occasions. She was lonely on most evenings and was thankful for Maya's company.

She was at her home watching her favorite tv show which, she was ashamed to admit to anyone, was Wheel of Fortune. She had plonked herself in front of the television, a cup of tea in her hand, watching the show intently. This was her idea of a perfect end to a hectic day at the hospital where she worked as a nurse in the Intensive Care Unit.

Her phone rang and she reluctantly picked it up.

"Shabnam, this is Maya. I am in deep trouble. I need to speak to you about something really important." Maya's voice at the other end sounded extremely urgent.

"What's going on?"

"I am not sure what's going on, but I think that Kunal is behaving in a very strange manner."

"What do you mean? He was fine when we just met last night."

"He is...I don't know...strangely different. He is talking to himself and he is pacing nonstop, he is not answering my questions. It is as if he is a different person altogether! He is acting as if he has not heard me, he is as if in a trance. I really do not know what to do!"

"Is your marriage ok? Is there anything going on?"

"What is that supposed to mean?" Maya asked furiously. *"I really need help. Can you be here as soon as possible?"*

She was hysterical as she told her what had happened. She begged her to come to the house and pick her and Sonu up, right away. She asked if it would be okay if they could spend the day with her.

Poor Sonu was only six years old at that time and was crying in confusion. He tried to wipe the blood from her face with his tiny hands. She heard the soft sobbing noise among his confused questions. His cries would stay etched in her mind forever.

As she left the house with Shabnam, she looked back at the birthday streamers and balloons still decorating the living room. She cast one lasting look around the house.

Kunal, her husband of seventeen years, was still mumbling to himself. At times, he was smiling at something in space through his delirium. His hands twitched periodically, his arms moving rapidly, waving off unseen objects in the air.

Maya called 911 from Shabnam's car. They waited till EMS arrived. Maya gave them her account of the events and watched them place Kunal in a stretcher and take him to the hospital. She did not mention her own injury to the emergency technicians at all.

CHAPTER
TWENTY TWO

DISTURBIA . . . 2004

Maya and Sonu stayed with Shabnam for the next two days.

Frantic phone calls were made to Maya's family and Kunal's father in India. Words of encouragement were floated around.

Maya's parents were supportive, but their advice seemed very irrelevant as she did not think they understood what was happening. She stopped talking to them about it as she knew they just could not fathom the seriousness of the situation. They had no idea what psychiatric illness really was. They offered her platitudes such as *"Make sure that Kunal gets his rest; take care of Sonu; do not stress Kunal too much about unimportant things; make sure you cook fresh chapattis for your father-in-law."*

Maya felt that they should have appeared more worried about the fact that Kunal had physically harmed her. That fact was lost in all the abundant words of advice that were given to her. They really had no clue about the complicated quagmire that her life had already become.

Her father-in-law flew over as soon as he could buy the next air ticket. He was very quiet on his arrival. He only smiled briefly when he met Sonu, his only grandson that he had seen for the first time in his life. He wanted to meet Kunal and speak to him as soon as possible. Kunal was still admitted to the psychiatric ward and no visitation was allowed for the next two days. Only two fifteen-minute phone calls were allowed on a daily basis.

He spoke to Kunal on the phone every day. In between those phone calls, he sat for hours on the couch thinking silently. Maya saw him listening to Kunal's limited conversation and observed a dark look of helplessness creep over his face at the end of each phone call. Maya sensed a deep, dark sadness in Kunal's father each time she looked at him. She also got an eerie feeling that he had been through this situation before.

He barely ate, stayed restless and almost had no sleep until he was finally allowed to visit Kunal at the hospital in two weeks. Kunal sent her a note through his father.

"Maya, please do not worry. I am getting better and will be home at the end of this week. My psychiatrist says that I suffered from a nervous breakdown, probably brought on by too much stress.

Give Sonu a kiss for me.

Dad appears very apprehensive, but he will be all right. He is a strong chap.

Take care of yourself.

Love

Kunal."

Maya felt that she had failed as a wife, as a woman, and as a mother. It was impossible for her to look at Sonu and not remember the night she had to leave the house with terror in his eyes. She was painstakingly reminded of the pity and sympathy that she saw in Shabnam's eyes that day. Her shame was absolute as she remembered herself breaking down and crying in front of Shabnam.

She still felt clueless and felt unable to look ahead and make any sense of her life. She was in a strange country far away from her parents. She was married to the man she had once loved. She had *cheated* on him and had injured his heart forever.

Now things were starting to go bad.

Bad karma had come back to reap toll from her.

CHAPTER

TWENTY THREE

I AM ALL RIGHT NOW . . . 2004

Kunal had assured her that this would not happen again and that he will do whatever it takes to keep the family together.

She wanted him to see a psychiatrist on a regular basis and he agreed. He actually wanted her to go with him to the appointments. He was diagnosed with a bipolar disorder and was started on psychiatric medications. Kunal started taking his medicines with diligence. He also went to his psychotherapy sessions and monthly follow ups regularly.

After continued treatment, Kunal's old self seemed to make a resurgence. He was visibly getting better. His eyes appeared tired at times, occasionally picturing the turmoil that he had been through, but he was better. He started going back to work and normalcy returned to their lives.

It seemed that he could now begin to laugh again, he was more regular with his sleep patterns and seemed to spend more time with Sonu guiding him in his homework, taking him to his soccer games and trips to the movies seemed to return to their life.

Even Sonu seemed to have a cautious smile on his face and the doubtful look with which he regarded his father seemed to be fading away.

Kunal's father stayed with them for three months and his mood improved as Kunal's health got better. He was proud of his son's achievements. He played with Sonu and spoilt him with expensive gifts and money. He thanked Maya for being an understanding and devoted wife.

Unknown even to Maya herself, something inside her broke irreparably the day Kunal had his nervous breakdown. Years from that day, she would still remember that incident, that very instant when Kunal had violently shoved her.

It was not so much his act of shoving her, but the expression of pure and evil hatred on his face scared her. She would never forget the crazed look on his face. That image lingered in her mind, etching itself deeper into her memory each passing minute, slowly spreading and expanding to engulf their lives completely.

Around that time, Maya started thinking about her career. She needed to have a job so that she could become financially independent.

"What would she do if Kunal attacked her again?"

The injury to Maya's forehead was minor. Still, she could not forget the violence of the action. She decided that she did not want to live in fear of physical violence.

She vowed to herself that when the time was *right,* she would *definitely* leave him.

Before Sonu's birth, she had not taken her old job seriously. Kunal was the major breadwinner in the family. Money was not a problem and they had a comfortable life even without Maya's salary. Once Sonu was born, she wanted to spend time at home and had no inclination to work anymore.

Her employment was terminated as she did not return to work after her six-month sabbatical was over.

Now, she really needed a job, *any job.*

After her father-in-law left for India, Maya started sending in her job applications.

CHAPTER TWENTY FOUR

MAYA AND SONU . . . 2004

It was the beginning of a very uneasy year for her.

She had not worked for six years (since Sonu's birth). Now, she *had* to find a way to get back into the workforce.

She was very doubtful of her ability to land a job. In spite of that, she made her resume and sent it to all the architectural firms that she could find in the yellow pages.

She made about twenty phone calls every day. After about a month of eager pursuit, the best she could do was to get an interview to work as a secretary at a small private firm in Schenectady, a city which was 45 minutes away from home.

She fished out her navy blue *"interview suit"* that she could barely fit into. She squeezed her feet into the unflattering pumps, drove for 45 minutes and showed up for the interview.

She was obviously overqualified for the job and the interviewer repeatedly asked her whether she was *sure* that she wanted this job. It would be nothing more than a secretarial position and there was not much potential for growth, and it was only 12 dollars an hour. She was almost *adamant* that she wanted the job. The violent fervor to work must have shone through her eyes convincingly.

Maya was hired on the spot and was instructed to go and meet with Joan, the HR (human resources) lady. Joan was also the current secretary, receptionist and biller *all in one*. Joan was planning to retire in a month and Maya would be taking over her job, she was informed.

Maya accepted the job right away and was instructed to start work as soon as her pre-employment physical was done.

She drove home prouder than she had ever felt in her entire life.

It was very clear that Kunal did not like her going to work. Especially, when all she did was purely secretarial work at the private architectural firm. He thought that she was overqualified for her job which mainly entailed making appointments, answering the phone, ordering coffee and lunch for her three bosses.

Occasionally, *very occasionally*, she would chip in her advice about certain projects. This was mostly smiled at and indulgingly dismissed by her superiors.

The senior most partner, Jim, an older white man had headed his private architectural firm for the last twenty years. He *never* took her advice. However, he always heard her ideas out as he nodded patiently at her. The other two partners were younger, more impatient and she was not even sure that they ever heard her entire sentence before dismissing her.

Kunal pointed her multiple times that he was making enough money for both of them and she really did not need to work. Each time Kunal criticized her job, Maya told him with a smile that she would never quit her job, even if she won the lottery!

She knew that even though he did not like it, Kunal understood her desire for independence. If nothing else, he respected her for that.

Two years passed by.

Maya had earned a raise at the end of each year and was now making 14 dollars an hour. She was very careful with her money and saved it, whenever possible. By the end of 2 years, she had saved about 20,000 dollars.

Kunal was still working and his behavior had not erupted at all. Actually, he was doing exceptionally well. His doctor visits were less frequent now. Soon, he was released from therapy as well.

Maya and Kunal started interacting with their friends. Once again, they were included in the social occasions in their community. Maya's embarrassment regarding her husband's psychiatric episode seemed to be receding and she was able to enjoy these evenings. She started to relish weekend evenings where she could meet her friends and talk about useless stuff such as movies, jewelry and fashion once again.

One day, Jim did not show up for work. His wife called and informed that he had suffered a major heart attack and had to be hospitalized. She wanted the office to close down

Jim's projects and requested that the other partners take them over.

Maya managed to convince her that she could supervise the projects that were in progress. She would try to keep the clients happy. If there were any issues, she assured Jim's wife, she would hand over the accounts to the other partners.

The wife agreed and thought that it was a great idea as Maya was a qualified architect.

Maya loved the month and a half that followed. She split her day into office work in the first half and site visits during the second half. It felt great to be on site, checking the blueprints and making sure that the specifications were met.

At times, she recognized fundamental errors in the designs and made minor changes to correct them. It was oddly empowering to act like a real architect for a while. Two of the projects were finished on schedule and there was an actual payment made for her work! Maya felt a rush of excitement when she received the check for the completed projects. She was as excited as a little child as she telephoned her boss, who was recuperating at home, to tell him about the payment.

That day, Jim offered her to work for the company as a junior architectural associate.

She was overjoyed.

As Maya stepped out of the office that afternoon to drive to Sonu's school to pick him up, she felt that she was holding her head higher and that there was a new meaning in every step she took.

The first thing Maya did was go shopping. She spent time looking for a more expensive work wardrobe. She ended up buying five good quality suits, five blouses, three pairs of shoes (black and brown pumps and flat walking shoes), scarves and a work bag. She brought out her textbooks and proudly arranged them on her work desk. She was nervous about the first job that was assigned to her. She drew up her plans and spent hours perfecting them. She was happy to realize that her education had not been in vain. Maya's confidence grew manifold with every project that she completed successfully.

Another conscious decision that she made was to never neglect Sonu. She made it clear to her boss that she needed to be involved in her son's upbringing and education. She offered to work weekends or from home in case she had to take time off for her son.

Her day started with taking Sonu to the preschool located close to her house. She had made a special effort to make friends with other parents and had offered to carpool. Maya was usually the one picking up other children from their homes to drive to the preschool and back. She did not mind doing more than her turns as she treasured the time, she spent with Sonu, anyways. It was helpful to know that if she ever was in a bind that she could rely on one of the other parents to pick Sonu up.

Kunal was always busy with his work and he would have made arrangements to change his routine if needed. Maya just did not want to bother him.

It was a joy for her to see Sonu grow into a very articulate youngster. He was enrolled into an expensive private school and the pictures from his first day in school in the customary school uniform made her cry. She volunteered in all the school activities, chaperoned camping trips and helped set up science fairs. She attended all of Sonu's little soccer league games, in which, sorrowfully, her son scored not a single goal. Maya went to his choir concerts where he was not the star singer, but a tiny voice from way back in the chorus line. She was part of the organizing committee for bake sales in the school even though her baking was pathetic; she bought the cookies from the local bakery and passed them on as *homemade*. She helped him with his homework.

She became a busy whirlwind of activity and kept herself busy. She kept Sonu as close to herself as possible. She was fearful of letting Sonu bear the brunt of Kunal's angry outbursts. She wanted to shield Sonu from any unpleasantness.

As Sonu got older, he was able to discern his father's behavior patterns. He noted that there was cycle of good days followed by bad. There were days when he smiled and laughed and was extremely loving. These days could go on for two or three months. This happy period was followed by about four or five days when he did not shower or shave or go to work. He did not eat his meals with them, stayed cooped up in his library and had to be coaxed by his mother to make an appointment with his doctor. Many times, he saw his mom drive him to the doctor's office after dropping him off to school.

Occasionally, his father was in the hospital and returned home after a few days. Sonu had become a little apprehensive of his father's illness. His personality seemed to swing between an extremely exceptional loving father and a complete stranger whose eyes did not recognize him for days. Initially, Sonu was very confused and felt that he had brought on the sudden outbursts of anger. Later, he understood that his father suffered from an illness and this was not his fault. His mother had explained the situation to him multiple times; she had even made appointments with a counselor for him and that had made it easier for him to cope with his father's illness.

Slowly, Sonu learnt to take these episodes in his stride. He had become good at gauging his father's moods. He stayed busy with his school, was happy to spend his time with his friends and his tutors as Maya had realized that she could not help with Sonu's homework after elementary school. The educational system was way too different from what she had experienced in India. The subject matter of fifth grade Math was new to her and she was not ashamed to admit that. She had hired instructors for Math and English.

As Sonu reached teenage years, Maya kept him busy and focused on his curriculum. Sonu had a good group of friends and he had indicated that he wanted to go to college on the West Coast. Maya did not want to have him go so far, but she did not want to become an obstacle in his dreams. She reminded him to stay committed to his studies and prepare well for his SATs and get an exceptional score.

Maya felt exhausted at times. She had decided never to complain about her life. She knew that her life had its unique set of challenges; but she still considered herself lucky to have enough financial means. She could easily afford Kunal's medical care, Sonu's education and still live a good life.

Kunal's business was doing very well and he had hired additional associates in his firm, guaranteeing a regular income.

When Maya was not exhausted, she was lonely. There were times when she longed for companionship. Her mind was restless at times and Kunal's hospitalizations took an emotional toll on her. Earlier, she had been completely focused on her work and Sonu's education. As Sonu became more independent, her mind began to wander. Maya began wondering about her friend's married lives.

"Were they all happy and content?"

Her *wanderlust* returned. She looked in the mirror one night and was dissatisfied with her reflection. She did not seem to have the magnetic attraction in her eyes anymore and her cheeks appeared sunken and hollow. Her sleepless nights showed in the dark circles beneath her eyes and her hair was streaked with strands of gray. She decided that very night, to put an end to her loneliness. She was not going to waste away.

The very next day, she saw her beautician, her manicurist and met her friend Shabnam for dinner. Shabnam could sense a change in Maya, though she could not really fathom her thoughts. She remarked, repeatedly, how youthful Maya looked that night.

Maya came back home emboldened and empowered. A few finishing touches were all that she required, and her mirror seemed to certify that she was still beautiful and desirable.

It was a shameful night when she slept with Sonu's tutor a week later.

However, Maya used her life situation as her armor and held herself defiant in the fact that she also deserved to be happy. There were many adulterous occasions that followed that night and Maya tried her best at keeping them discreet and away from Sonu's knowledge.

There was always a cheery mood to her tone now, which irritated Kunal persistently.

Maya's late nights had started again. Kunal, was starting to become unhappy again.

Maya's absences from home, stories about going and working at a homeless shelter to help people *(ha, please!!!)*, office get-togethers and client meetings became more frequent.

"How he longed for being able to trust her again!

CHAPTER TWENTY FIVE

O, SWEET MOTHER OF MINE . . . 2018

Kunal had no memory of how his aimless driving amid his rambling thoughts brought him to his office.

He was still numb as he entered through the front door. He instructed Lisa, his secretary, to clear his schedule and to give the rest of his staff a day off. Kunal explained to Lisa that he wanted to go over some legal paperwork and did not want any distractions.

He asked Lisa to brew a large pot of coffee. He took off his suit jacket and loosened his tie as he flopped into his chair. He assured Lisa that he was going to be all right, as she questioningly pointed out that he was still wearing the same clothes as yesterday.

He smiled warily at her and waved her off as she peeked into his room one last time before she left.

He sat down at his table with the voices in his head getting louder by the minute.

"Maya was asking for a divorce!"

"How was that even possible?"

"How will I live?"

"Was everything not going well for them?"

"Why now?"

"Why?"

Involuntarily, his mind raced to the time when his mother passed away, many, many years ago, when he was in college. He could remember the sequence of events in his mind clearly, each moment unfolding in front of his eyes, as if it had just happened yesterday.

Kunal's mother was diagnosed with a severe case of epilepsy. There were times when she was unresponsive from her attacks for a prolonged duration, sometimes hours, even longer. She had to be hospitalized on multiple occasions.

When the episode was over, and she returned home from hospital, she was back to complete normalcy. It was a contrast as stark as night and day.

After her recovery, when she came back home, the whole house buzzed with a happy energy. Right from the very first day when she came back from the hospital, she made herself busy with the neglected household chores. She instructed the servants to buy groceries, would cook and clean the house. She was bubbly and cheerful. Right away, she entered the kitchen and started cooking with gusto. It gave her immense pleasure to cook Kunal's favorite foods.

Unfortunately, Kunal had watched this pattern over and over. He remembered feeling sad whenever she was at the hospital.

He could clearly recall the very first episode of her illness.

He was only 5 years old. He was crying in his room after leaving his mother at the hospital. He found it very strange that his mother was not there to give him his meal at night or to read him his favorite story. When he woke up in the morning, there was no fragrance of incense purifying the house. There was no sound of her singing and praying in her little temple room. He particularly missed the melody of *bhajan* glorifying Lord Krishna and the random ringing of the little bell that she liked to intersperse the songs with.

She was not there to help him with his bath, change his clothes or to tell him to eat his eggs *(if he wanted to become big and strong!)*. There was no one to tell him to come inside the house when it became infernally hot during the summer afternoons.

Without her, there were no rules, no routine or structure to his days. He felt that days were never ending. Time stretched and expanded without any tangible boundaries. He felt suspended in a strange space, an empty void of timelessness.

At times, he would wake up at night, sobbing and looking for his mother.

When her seizures became more frequent, and if the hospitalization extended for more than a few days, Kunal's father requested his younger sister to help them.

At those times, there was a new routine. He would be woken up by his aunt who was nice but could never sound like his mother. She was always dressed in white. He found out that the reason was that she was a widow, as her husband had died a few years ago.

Her food did not taste the same as his ma's food.

He ate it *anyhow*.

He did not particularly like it when his aunt tried to kiss or hug him. He let her do that anyways thinking that it pleased her.

Most of all, he did not like it when she used his mother's temple. In the morning, she prayed to the same gods as her mother; the chants and the *bhajans* were the same but they did not sound the same.

The words were there but the *melody* was gone.

He pretended to like them anyways.

He remembered bowing his head in the temple and asking God to send his mother home as soon as possible so that his aunt would go away.

His entire childhood was plagued by such occurrences, and his mother was at the hospital almost every month for about five days. She was at the hospital when he won his first cricket match in second grade; when he won the first prize for his debate for equality for women in eighth grade and when he won a scholarship for the model for a solar home designed by him and his best friend in high school.

She was also in hospital when he had his first fight in eighth grade with a boy who called his mother a *mental patient*. She never learnt that he had hit that boy's head with a large rock and knocked him unconscious for *two hours*.

She would also never know of the instance when his aunt had cut herself with a knife while chopping onions in the kitchen. Kunal had stared at the blood gushing out of her wound, *fascinated* by how red her blood was as it dripped onto the floor in a puddle.

He was strangely *disappointed* when the bleeding stopped after she put a bandage on it.

Kunal's mother also did not know that he had visions of her every single night that she was at the hospital. He could hear her talking, her gentle voice sometimes becoming strangely urgent. Mostly she would tell him to do his homework, or to shower and get ready.

Once in a while, he was woken up from sleep seeing her writhing in a seizure, unconscious, foaming at the mouth, a shrill scream escaping her lips through a clenched jaw. It took him a few minutes to differentiate his nightmare from reality.

At those times, Kunal lay in his bed shaking, sweating, alone and scared.

Kunal did not bother his father with his nightmares. Kunal's father was a gentle soul who was constantly unhappy and burdened by his wife's condition. Even when his mother was well, he would see a look of masked apprehension on his face.

Those days from old played in front of Kunal's eyes as a faded black and white movie. His mind continued to drift aimlessly, switching between past and present.

His reverie was broken by the sound of his cell phone ringing.

"Hey dad! How are you?" Sonu's voice came across the phone.

"Good, son! Very good! When are we going to see you?"

"How is Mom?"

A few beads of sweat broke onto Kunal's brow and a strange chill shook his entire body. He was shaking. He had some calls to make but he could not think clearly.

"Sonu will be arriving tomorrow."

He had to break the news of their impending divorce to him.

He had to get back home, but he could not even get his legs to move.

"This is not going to be easy," he thought to himself.

CHAPTER

TWENTY SIX

DON'T WAKE UP
THE DEAD . . . 2018

Somehow, Kunal made himself get up. He switched his office lights off, packed the divorce papers into his briefcase, set the security code and walked into the parking lot of his office.

He looked back at his office, a multistoried building with dark glass facades, steel pillars framing the angles of the structure. The entire building was constructed so that it appeared to lean forward, and the topmost level was angled upwards from the flanks. It was an architectural expression of a bird about to soar into flight.

His heart always filled up with pride whenever he looked at his office. Today, he experienced no elation upon looking at his creation. Instead, an empty, hollowness spread into the abysmal darkness of his heart.

"I have a thousand things to take care of," Kunal reminded himself.

He got into his Mercedes and started the engine to go home.

Again, his mother's voice was in his head. He could hear her saying *"Don't worry. Everything is going to be all right."*

Kunal remembered when he was accepted to the DAC (Delhi Architectural College). He was overjoyed, and he had run home from his friend's house to let his parents know. He knew that his father would be ecstatic, and his mother would promptly run to her temple to thank her collection of gods.

Instead, his mother started crying. She held on to Kunal and started sobbing, lamenting the fact that he would move away from her and that she will never see him again. His heart grew soft and for a moment his happiness was diminished.

Eventually however, after hugging him a million times, and making him promise that he will fly over to see her every three months, and that he will call her every day, she was ready to celebrate. She sped to the kitchen to start making sweet treats for him.

The next day, she had an extralong prayer session with her gods and entire divinity was invoked to shower Kunal with blessings and to provide him with protection from all sorts of evil.

Kunal had seen her joyous face and remembered comparing it to the contorted version that it assumed when she lay unconscious in the middle of a seizure. It almost made him angry that she had to have such a terrible illness.

Kunal had wished wistfully for his mother to always look like that, the happy and exuberant version of herself.

When he was at college, he had called her regularly. He had not told his friends about his mother's illness. He was embarrassed by it, as if it was a stigma and a shameful secret that he had to endure. He did not want anyone to know the ugly version of his mother, convulsing, lying helpless on the bed, at times covered in her vomit or urine.

Even Maya did not know about his mother's illness.

CHAPTER

TWENTY SEVEN

YOU ARE THE FIRST AND THE LAST . . . 1984

"Ah, Maya!!"

"How madly he had fallen in love with her!"

Even before Kunal realized what love truly meant, he was head over heels in love with Maya. It was not just a passing fancy or a simple lighthearted crush on a girl. He had never felt so helplessly in love with anyone before.

Kunal vividly remembered his first meeting with Maya in college. He remembered how she looked in the pale pink outfit that she wore that day. She had glowing skin, shiny hair and a smile that seemed to make her eyes sparkle. Her movements were smooth, and her voice was covered with velvet. She was not one of the loud-mouthed girls who believed that they had to be loud and high-pitched to be considered hip and modern. She was comfortable in traditional attire and looked simply ravishing.

He remembered being her partner in the introductory course in the first semester. He was so shy and had taken too long to confess his feelings for her. If he could do it all over again, he would never have wasted so much time thinking and rethinking about how he was going to approach her, just to let her know that he liked her.

His friends were typical nineteen-year-old hormonal animals! They only wanted to be seen with a girl so that they could appear cool and brag about it in the boy's hostel.

He did not want to do that. Maya deserved better and he was going to wait until the time felt right before he attempted to divulge his feelings to her.

How could he make her realize what he felt whenever he saw her?

How could he make her understand that from dawn till dusk, he thought only of her?

How could he tell her that she was the reason he sometimes forgot to call his mother?

Kunal felt as if all the synapses in his brain, his conscious and unconscious mind were completely saturated with thoughts of her. It was pure happiness to meet her in class and revel in those moments for the rest of the day. Even a trivial meeting with her acquired a whole new meaning and became a significant memory. It was as if there was a movie playing in Kunal's head and Maya was always the *star*. She was eternally smiling in that role.

Kunal was very happy living like this, completely and totally obsessed with Maya.

His friends were a little worried at times.

He was a little *too deep into her*, they said.

"And when are you actually going to let her know that she is the lucky one?"

"And how old will you be when you finally ask her out to a cup of coffee?"

"How many years since you set eyes on her, is it twenty?"

"If I were you, we would be married already and on our honeymoon!!"

"Did you see how she looked at you today during class?"

"I think you should ask her out right now!"

"You are right. She is too good for you."

"I think something is wrong with you."

"Come on, man. Get talking to her already."

They were always silenced by the same response every time.

"Don't worry. I will ask her when the time is right. And no, I am not gay! Also, I am not suffering from E.D. If you don't believe me, set me up with your sister and she can let you know the truth."

By the end of the first year, Maya and Kunal were part of the same group of friends but they were still not *officially* dating.

CHAPTER
TWENTY EIGHT

THE PHONE CALL . . . 1985

Kunal vividly remembered the day he got the phone call. The peon from his principal's office came to his class and informed him that the principal wanted him to come to his office right away.

When he reached his office, the principal was holding the phone for him.

"Your father, Mr. Sinha, is on the line."

"Kunal beta, your mother is not doing well. She is in the hospital, and I would like you to come over right away. I will wire you the money for the ticket. Please take the next flight out from Delhi to Bombay. Can you do that?"

"Sure. I will head to the airport right now." Kunal shivered inwardly as he left the office.

He knew that something was terribly wrong. His mother was probably deteriorating. He ran to the boys' hostel, picked up his clothes and shoved them into a suitcase. He grabbed all the money he had. He ran and got into a taxi and arrived at the airport. The next flight was in six hours.

He sat at the airport, worrying that he might doze off and miss the flight. He had not been sleeping well. His midterm exams were due soon and he had been studying late into the night.

He slept in fits as he waited at the airport gate, waking up occasionally, disoriented and wondering where he was.

He dreamt that he had missed the flight, failed his exams and that his mother had recovered entirely from her illness and he was driving her home.

Kunal boarded the flight and was in Bombay at noon. He called his father from the airport. His father sent his car and driver to pick Kunal up from the airport and bring him straight to the hospital.

When Kunal arrived at the hospital, he was inwardly reluctant to go in. He did not want to see his mother struggling with her illness again, her face contorting with the onslaught of uncontrollable convulsions.

He had a strange feeling, almost like *de-ja-vu*. He had done this too many times in the past. He was walking in a surreal world, suspended in an unpleasant dream. He had to touch the hospital gate to make sure that he was not dreaming.

His father met him at the hospital entrance and walked with him to his mother's room. As Kunal was about to enter the room, his father put his arm around Kunal, as if protecting him from what he was about to see. It was as if he did not want him to go inside the room, just yet.

"She had another seizure three days ago and she has still not opened her eyes. Dr Narayanan thinks that this time she may have suffered brain damage from lack of oxygen. She may not recognize you; I just want you to know that." Kunal's father sounded grave and spoke in a voice devoid of all hope.

When Kunal entered the room, he was shocked. His mother was hooked up to IV fluids, a heart monitor was attached to her chest and an endotracheal tube was inserted in her mouth along with a nasogastric tube in her nasal cavity. She had been placed on the ventilator, which was breathing for her. She was sedated with the help of morphine and did not even know that he was there.

Kunal was heartbroken. He was prepared for the worst, but he had not imagined his mother to be like this.

He could not find the beauty in her face that he remembered and cherished so dearly. Her smiling face and loving eyes that brought him peace and made him feel that he was the source of her happiness had been replaced by a swollen, lifeless face colored by the shadows of death. He looked at her puffy, unconscious face; her half-closed stuporous eyes, her bruised arms and her helpless, almost lifeless body attached to the ventilator. The ventilator made a hissing sound with every breath that it delivered into her lungs.

Kunal's eyes involuntarily turned away from that sight.

Occasionally, his mother's body jerked uncontrollably as her seizures were still not fully controlled in spite of sedation. However, these were just a few twitching movements; not the violent *grand mal* shakes that Kunal saw as a child. Each time that happened, a nurse would run in the room and make a note in the chart and push some medicine into her vein.

Kunal became dizzy and turned to leave the room. His father met him at the door and suggested that he should go home and get some rest. His father's driver took him home in the car and he reached home.

Once again, he was home, and his mother was away at the hospital. Only this time, there was no knowing whether she was going to ever return.

Kunal went to his room which appeared very different from when he had left. The room had been freshly painted and had new curtains. His posters of favorite rock bands "Guns N' Roses and Aerosmith" were no longer there. There were strange clothes hanging in his closet, he noted absentmindedly. He lay down on the bed and closed his eyes. He was exhausted and overcome by sadness. The old memories of nights spent in the house while his mother was in the hospital came back.

He went to bed crying, his tears soaking into the bedsheets.

When he woke up, Kunal headed to the shower. Their old housemaid, Kamla came to greet him. She looked much older than before. Kamla looked at him with sad eyes and asked him to come to the dining room for dinner after his shower. He nodded silently. After a hot shower, he changed into fresh clothes and sat at the dining table.

Kamla was waiting for him, with fresh chapati and *daal* and his favorite dish of *aaloo matar curry*.

"Kamla, whose clothes are in my closet?"

"Oh, those are Sushma auntie clothes. Many time she come over to help bibiji if see get too sick or if see come back from the hospital." Kamla insisted on speaking to him in her broken English.

Sushma auntie was a good friend of the family. She had recently widowed as her husband had passed away due to cancer. It seemed a little odd to Kunal that she would come and stay for the night at their house. Apparently, his mother was not doing well at all lately and had to have more help than before.

"And what happened to Mummyji this time? How did she get so sick all of a sudden?"

"Well, it happened last Shaturrday. I go to my house after around 8 pm on Friday. Bibiji had eaten her dinner and was looking happy. When I come back the next mornin and go to her room I see that she breathing very bad. She not wake up when I call her, and she vomiting all over her clothes. Then I ran to Sahib's room to call Sushma auntie to help and then we call ambulance and take her to hospital. Poor bibiji, I hope she come home all better."

"So Sushma auntie was not in Mummyji's room...?"

"No baba. She mostly in Sahib's room," Kamla said in a very embarrassed tone.

Kunal was disconcerted when he understood the implied meaning. He felt heated blood rising to his cheeks and his fists clenching in anger. He could not eat another bite of food or swallow a drink of water.

He packed his bag and told Kamla that he was going to the hospital to be with his mother and that he might just sleep there that night.

"Baba, at least finish your dinner..."

He slammed the door and left.

CHAPTER
TWENTY NINE

HOW CAN I LEAVE YOU
AGAIN . . . ? 1985

As Kunal sat at his mother's bedside, his studies, his college life and everything else appeared to be immaterial to him. It seemed as if his exams, dreams of being an architect, even Maya existed in a different universe altogether. It was as if he had been transported to a remote, distant planet disconnected from everything else.

All that seemed to matter was that his mother was struggling to stay alive...and his *father was a cheater!*

It was hard to come to terms with that. If he thought any longer about that, he could hurt someone and cause a major problem. Each time he thought of his father, he felt like taking an axe and splitting him right down the middle, and he also pictured doing the same thing to his once favorite Sushma auntie.

He knew that he should not think like that. Maybe, there was be a perfectly rational explanation for Sushma auntie to be in their house.

All he wanted to do was to hold his enfeebled mother in his arms and take her to a place far away where she would be healthy and happy.

Kunal wished wistfully that he could make her seizures go away; give her all the years back free from the disease that had so plagued her life.

How few were the times when she was healthy!

How often had she lived under the shadow of disaster waiting to happen!

How few were the occasions when she had dressed up, gone shopping or thrown house parties like the other moms that he knew in the neighborhood!

The threat of having a seizure anytime had limited her life so much. The embarrassing spectacle of laying on the floor convulsing, foaming at the mouth and losing control of her bladder and stools in front of others was just too much for her to cope with.

Kunal's father was also aware of the social humiliation that her *medical problem* could cause and occasionally let her know that in so many words.

She was so helpless, as she lay in her hospital bed, unresponsive, innumerable medications pumping into her while the ventilator hissed meaningless breath into her lungs. She was not a pretty sight to look at. At times, the unpleasant sight of her bedclothes covered in human waste, her shriveling limbs and the smell of antiseptic mixed with urine and stools was too much to bear for Kunal. She was now developing a bedsore that was starting to fester. Kunal could not feel anything but anger and frustration mixed with immeasurable sadness each time he looked at her.

Yet, he loved her so much and wanted to protect her. He wanted to save her from the ugly and helpless state that she was in, but he was equally helpless himself.

He was by her bedside dozing off when he heard his father's voice.

"Kunal beta! You should go home and get some rest. You have been here all night. Now, I am here, and I will stay till evening."

Kunal shook his head wordlessly and stared at his father with strange eyes. His gaze appeared to pierce through his father's body as if focusing at a miniscule point at the wall behind him. He was overcome by hatred for his father. Anger and helplessness choked him in his throat, and he could not bring himself to speak a single word.

His father was taken aback when he saw the icy look in Kunal's eyes that glared at him accusingly. He almost took a step back, steadied himself as he stepped towards him.

Kunal stayed seated in his chair, held up his hand with his finger pointing at his father, wordlessly threatening him for a long time. Then he leaned back into the chair, covered his face with his hands and rested his head on his mother's bed.

His father tried to console Kunal but Kunal violently pushed him back with his right arm. His father turned and left the room, confused at Kunal's reaction. He went down to the cafeteria, picked up coffee and some food and left it by Kunal's chair.

His father pulled up a chair next to Kunal's and wordlessly watched moments from his wife's life ticking away.

A whole week passed and Kunal's mother had shown no signs of improvement. The seizures had become less frequent, but they never ceased completely.

Finally, the neurologist had a meeting with the family and suggested that all aggressive treatment be withdrawn. In his opinion, she was way past the possibility of making any meaningful recovery. He thought that it would be kinder to her if the family agreed to have the ventilator removed and to let her pass. He patted Kunal's father sympathetically on his shoulder as he told him to prepare for the worst.

Kunal's father did not want to give up yet. He wanted to try for about another week and see if Kanta, his wife of forty-five years, could recover enough to at least bring her home. He did not want her to die in the hospital.

Kunal, however, held a different opinion. He did not want her to suffer any more. According to him, she had suffered enough already, and he just wanted her to be comfortable. The body that was attached to a ventilator and appeared disfigured and lifeless to him already. He could not call *that* his mother. Her face contorted with every breath that the ventilator puffed into her chest. Her limbs were entangled into multiple intravenous lines. He looked and looked at her face and could not find any beauty emanating from it. He felt revolted by the ugly spectacle of her mother in the hospital bed in front of him.

"Well, I am her husband and I really would like to try and see how she is going to do in a week. I am not ready to give up on her yet," Kunal's father told the doctor with finality.

"Funny, you should say that. I thought that you gave up on her already!"

– 147 –

"What do you mean?"

"You know what I mean. Ever wondered how she felt while you had your girlfriend in the house all the time?"

"Son, you mind your tongue. You cannot talk to me like that. What do you really mean?"

Kunal's father's tone got higher by the minute.

"Go ahead. Tell me that it is not true. Tell me that you were not shacking up with Sushma auntie. I saw her clothes all over the house. When exactly did she move in? Poor, poor Mummy," Kunal broke down sobbing.

"It is nothing like that. That is the problem with your generation. All you think about is…anyways, I do not have to give you any justifications."

"You are the one who has no morals, strange that I should be saying that to you," shouted Kunal with all his might.

"Well," Kunal's father said hesitatingly, looking for words while trying to keep his anger in check. *"Let's decide what is important right now. I have the power of attorney over your mother. I want to see if she is going to improve over the next week and make some arrangements for that. Hopefully she will get better and come home soon."*

"I hope she dies before she goes back to that godforsaken house, where you insulted her by bringing another woman into the house," Kunal yelled.

In blinding anger, Kunal grabbed the pen knife from his father's pocket. He removed the cover and stabbed his father in the arm. He withdrew the knife and attacked again and again. When blood started seeping above into Kunal's father's white shirt, Kunal finally stopped. His crazed eyes were hypnotized, staring fascinatingly at the blood slowly rising into the fabric and dripping on to the floor.

Kunal threw the knife on the floor and left the room.

Kunal called his childhood friend, Avinash and told him to come over and pick him up from the hospital. He asked Avi if he could stay at his house while he was in town. Avi watched his best friend from childhood sobbing uncontrollably. Kunal could barely speak comprehensibly but he told Avi that he just *could not* go back to his own house, not *just yet.*

The next few days were tense.

Kunal's father, who now had a large bandage on his left shoulder from severe lacerations caused by Kunal's attack, was extremely upset with Kunal's behavior. He tried to talk to him on multiple occasions.

Kunal, on the other hand, shunned his father completely.

In the entire universe he wanted to change only one thing and that was to make his mother healthy and he did not have the power to do that. Kunal felt the minuteness of his existence and a feeling of apathy took over him.

"How helpless I really am!" thought Kunal.

Kunal was at his mother's bedside constantly. The only time he left his mother's side was to go to a nearby temple to pray. He had never been the one to pray much before, but now he went to the temple every day without fail, just to quieten the noise in his turbulent mind. He could follow some of the prayer songs from his childhood; memories of his mother singing the same *bhajans* flooded his mind, but they did not sound as sweet.

Going to the temple made Kunal calmer and made it easier for him to go back to the hospital and be with his mother.

"A little bit of divine assistance helps at times like this," he thought to himself jeering at his own weakness.

The priest saw him come to the temple at odd hours and singled him out one day.

"What are you praying for, son?" he asked gently.

"My mother. She is very sick and is in the hospital," Kunal said bursting in tears, involuntarily.

The priest said sympathetically, *"Take this to her, son. This will give her some peace."*

He gave *'gangajal'* to him in a small tumbler.

"Wet her lips with this and sprinkle on her face every day and hopefully she will have 'shanti'. Have this so that you can experience peace as well," said the priest as he gave him some *'prasad'* to eat.

It was a strange experience for him, as he thanked the priest and wiped his tears.

Yet, with the small cup of *gangajal* in his hand, he felt strangely empowered. Yes, there was something he could do for her. He hoped that the sacred *gangajal* will provide her mother's soul peace and help her with her oncoming journey into the unknown. Maybe, by sprinkling the holy water, his mother's next life would be a more peaceful one.

Kunal was a staunch agnostic and he was aware that his action was neither logical nor reasonable. For him, it was difficult to understand the comfort devoted believers experienced by honoring age-old religious symbols. His mother, on the other hand, was a fervent believer in God and ancient Hindu customs.

Therefore, for his mother's sake, he visited the temple every day and sprinkled the holy water on her lips and forehead. He waited for the priest to give him *prasad* so that he could touch the holy food to her lips.

"Maybe, the blessings from the priest will ease her pain."

CHAPTER THIRTY

DEATH BE A LADY
TONIGHT!!! 1985

In spite of the fervent religious efforts on Kunal's part, his mother's condition declined steadily. She was slipping deeper and deeper into a coma. Her face had acquired a deathly expression.

There was nothing beautiful left in those cheeks that used to readily dimple into a smile. Her eyes that had once possessed a radiant light, were now dark and lifeless. Her soft hands that had touched his face in an ever-adoring manner were now withered and stiffened into claws. A deep darkness occupied the hollows of her cheeks. Flesh was melting away from her limbs and her skeleton peeked through her wasting body.

Kunal saw an ugly face when he looked at his mother. Her mouth was stretched in a tight grimace, her yellowing skin barely outlining the underlying bones. He still loved his mother, but the horridness of seeing her dying body was revolting.

His father, wanted to continue with the macabre, ugly display of her slow, torturous death. Kunal hated the fact that his father could not see that prolonging his mother's life at this stage was equivalent to inflicting more torment upon her. His hatred for his father grew every day.

Eighteen days had passed since his mother had been hospitalized. Kunal had been at his mother's bedside, relentlessly waiting for the faintest glimmer of hope. She showed no signs of improvement. Her seizures had stopped now. Her blood pressure was marginal.

Kunal had waited and waited for her to improve and now he could not wait any longer. If she had to die, he wanted her to die *already*. Kunal wanted the ridiculous, ugly spectacle, that had shorn his mother of her dignity, to be over as soon as possible.

That day he went to the temple and prayed to all the gods that he could remember.

He did not pray for her eyes to open and shine on him.

That day, he prayed *neither* for his mother's life *nor* for her peace or grace to be bestowed on her soul.

Kunal prayed in a weary, defeated voice, for his dear mother's *death*.

Kunal was tired just by watching his mother suffer. His mother was probably a hundred times as tired. Kunal really wanted her misery to end. He knew his father was not going to budge from his decision of waiting for another week.

Unless Kunal took matters in his own hands, that limp body that was once his mother, would continue to suffer.

She would remain an ugly spectacle drenched in her own urine and stools. When their relatives came to visit her at her bedside, they were not able to stand there long without delicately averting their noses.

He *had* to do something to save her dignity.

The thought reverberated in his head repeatedly.

He might have to *kill the flame for the fire was long gone.*

Normally, Kunal's father came to the hospital at 10 pm to spend the night at the hospital. After that, Kunal would silently gather his stuff and go to the parking lot where their driver waited for him. Every night Kunal went to Avi's house to catch some sleep.

Every night the driver asked the same question, *"Baba, won't you go to your own house? Sahib ji would feel very happy if you do that."*

"Not tonight, Randheer Singh. Maybe tomorrow night", Kunal promised every night.

"Ok Baba, as you wish."

That night, when Kunal's father came to the hospital at 10 pm, Kunal could see that his father looked extremely tired. Kunal continued to gaze at him as if he had seen him after an entire lifetime. This ordeal had taken a toll on him as well and for a brief moment, Kunal pitied him.

Quickly, he put his thoughts aside.

"Why don't you go home, dad, and sleep comfortably tonight?" Kunal asked his father.

"No, Kunal beta. You must be so tired. You have been at her bedside all day. I am actually worried about you. Go home beta, rest in your room and we can talk about whatever is troubling you," his father said imploringly.

"I will. Just let me sleep here tonight. I will be home tomorrow morning and we can have breakfast together," Kunal smiled his winning smile at his father through his tired eyes.

He had not spoken to his father since his outburst a week ago.

That little exchange made his father happy; a mixture of relief and joy broke into his face.

He came up to Kunal, held him by his shoulders and took one last look at the comatose, wasted figure that once was his wife and Kunal's mother. Tears welled up into his eyes as he turned and left the room.

"OK. You sleep here tonight, but I will wait for you, beta, in the morning. Everyone misses you at the house. Kamla is waiting to feed you your favorite foods. I will stay here during the day tomorrow. Do you promise that you will come home tomorrow, beta?"

"I will, dad. Have a good night."

Kunal was familiar with the nursing staff by now. The nurse on duty that night was Sister Reena, a young; about twenty-one years old. She was very efficient at her job and extremely helpful. She answered all of Kunal's questions with a lot of patience. She also supplied him with coffee whenever he asked for it.

Day after day, night after night, Sister Reena had seen the father and son at Kanta's bedside. It made her sad to see Kunal's agonizing thoughts etched on his face. She had spoken to him on multiple occasions, attempting to distract him from the constant worry that afflicted him. She would make small talk about the weather or an ongoing cricket match.

There were times when Kunal did not care to talk much and her chatter was just an annoyance. Yet, sometimes, it was a relief to be able to speak to someone. There were not that many questions he had about his mother anymore.

He knew that his mother was dying. Actually, in his mind, she was already *dead*. He knew she was suffering a slow undignified death.

"Not anymore," thought Kunal. *"Her misery would soon be over."*

He had a plan!

He went over his plan multiple times as he waited eagerly for the night nurse to arrive. He had even thought out the conversation that he was going to have with her tonight. When Sister Reena came to the room at the beginning of her shift, she checked his mother's vital signs and temperature. Her clinical condition was the same as compared to the night before. Kanta lay on the hospital bed suspended between life and death.

"She appears more dead than alive," Kunal thought to himself almost cynically.

He hated himself for being so crass. However, there was nothing beautiful about waiting for death to arrive. He despised his mother for putting him through this.

"How are you doing today, Sister Reena?" he asked. (In the hospital all nurses were addressed as "sister.")

"I am fine, Mr. Kunal. Do you want me to bring you some coffee? I just made a fresh pot," she smiled at him flashing her smile.

. *"Oh, thank you so much. I would love to have a cup, no cream or sugar. I am planning to stay here tonight and do some reading."* Kunal

pointed to the rather thick book that he had in his hands–
Towards a New Architecture by Le Corbusier.

"That seems very technical to me," she said looking quizzically at the cover.

"I am sure that your books would seem just as technical to me!" Kunal smiled one of his rare smiles at her.

"Did you already have dinner?" he asked her.

She was visibly surprised by his extra friendly behavior.

"Yes, I ate at home before I started for my shift. I usually eat at home with my family before I leave for work."

"That is nice," he said trying to imagine a happy family meal, something his own family will never ever have again.

"Are you going to have a busy night?"

"Yes, I need to stay awake. We are getting quite a few admissions tonight."

"Oh, well. You should not worry about my mother. She should be all right. She has been stable for a few nights now. I will come and call you if there is any problem."

"Oh, thank you. Let me get the coffee."

She sped through the hallway and brought him a steaming cup of fresh coffee. He smiled at her, leaned back into the chair and opened his book.

During the last two weeks, he had pocketed the extra vials of potassium chloride along with syringes and needles that the nurses had left carelessly in the room. All these items were hidden away in his bag. He was well prepared to carry out his plan. Kunal looked at his watch. It was almost midnight. He had three more hours. That was when the staff would be at its sleepiest.

Oddly, he felt a wave of excitement searing through him!

He stayed awake without any difficulty till 2 am. As the minutes ticked away, his eyelids grew heavier. He got up to use the bathroom. He saw that the nurses were busy in a new patient's room. He could see that they were administering CPR to the patient. He watched the ICU doctor giving orders and the nurses frantically carrying them out.

Kunal walked to the bathroom and splashed cold water on his face. He loaded all the vials of potassium chloride in a large syringe. An overdose of potassium chloride will cause the heart to stop, he had heard the nurses say. He changed the needle and walked back to his mother's bedside. He held the iv tubing, kinking it with his left hand and plunged the needle into the iv port. He had seen the nurses inject medications in the iv line on multiple occasions.

He emptied the entire syringe into the iv and released the tubing. He put the empty vials back in his pocket and threw the syringe in the trash can.

Nobody seemed to have noticed him. After he completed his evil task, he sank into his chair, frightened and exhilarated at the same time.

He watched the heart monitor, and *nothing* happened. The heartbeat tracing was unchanged.

He put his head down on the bed, pretending to be asleep. He looked up after a few minutes and there was still no change in the heartbeat. He was disappointed, again, getting restless with every passing second.

In about ten minutes, the heartbeat started to slow down. Eventually, even to his untrained eye, the heartrate became dangerously low on the monitor. All sorts of alarms went off and a code blue was sounded. Quickly, the room crowded with nurses along with the ICU doctor. The head nurse instructed Kunal to leave the room, explaining to him that there had been a critical change in his mother's condition. She told Kunal to call his father and suggested that he should come to the hospital as soon as possible.

He stepped out of the room looking appropriately shocked. He was oddly satisfied when he saw the flat line on the monitor. His mother's body was an ugly, lifeless heap, crumpled into the hospital bed. Kunal averted his eyes from the revolting sight.

The ICU doctor was now in the room. Kunal was helped into the family waiting area by one of the nurses. She brought him water and asked him if he needed anything. He silently shook his head. It was almost 4 am. Kunal stepped out into the hallway and called his father from the phone. His father answered the phone after the first ring as if he was expecting an ominous phone call.

"I will be right there," he said. *"Don't worry about anything, I will be there in 20 minutes."*

Kunal felt sad now, he could still see the nurses working on his mother in the room. He saw the monitor was still registering a flat line and he knew that pretty soon they will stop these efforts to revive her.

He felt a trickle of sweat from his forehead, a faint dizziness took over him and he swayed a little on his feet. The head nurse saw him swaying and was instantly at his side steadying him. She took him to the nearest chair and told him to keep his head down. He was given some more fluids to drink. Kunal had a fleeting glimpse of his mother's distorted face and he almost threw up.

When his father arrived, the ICU doctor came to the room to declare his mother dead. They removed her from the ventilator and covered her face with a white sheet.

NOW THAT I HAVE TASTED BLOOD . . . 1985

The funeral was a very solemn affair. All the relatives who lived close by, arrived at their house. As was customary, the women wore white clothes to express their grief at the sorrowful occasion. There was a lot of crying and hugging. Aunts and uncles who had not seen them for years, came to attend the funeral.

There were so many people in the house that Kunal's father had to hire a caterer to provide food at all the meals. Endless cups of tea were served, and everyone fondly remembered anecdotes regarding Kunal's mother. They highlighted and praised her good nature and generosity. They remembered her kindness on many occasions and glorified the goodness of her heart.

Kunal looked at her temple that housed her various gods. It was now completely neglected. There was no fragrant incense in the air and no singing of bhajans. Her mother's presence alone had made the temple holy and the air around it, sacred. With her death, it appeared as if the gods in the temple had also died. The temple, that was once alive due to her piety, had become ugly and lifeless, just like his mother's body.

His father wanted Kunal to join the menfolk and go to the cremation ground. According to Hindu tradition, his mother's body had to be cremated, to achieve liberation of the soul from mortal chains. His mother's body was placed on a wooden board. Her body was bathed with holy water and then a colorful sari was draped around it. Her funeral pyre was decorated with marigold flowers. Only her face was visible amid the flowers and it looked almost beautiful, certainly less distorted with pain and discomfort as compared to before. Now that she was out of the hospital, her face seemed rested. The reflected hues from pink and white roses mingled with golden tones from the marigold garlands and lent a healthy complexion to her cheeks.

He was in the front of the funeral procession. One of the four posts of the *arthi* rested on his right shoulder. Amidst the chanting of *"Ram naam satya hai,"* the funeral procession made their way to the cremation grounds. A pyre had been set up with logs of *Chandan* wood.

The heat from the setting sun made him sweat and several waves of dizziness came over Kunal. He tried to resist the desire to put the weight down and just run away.

It was a hurried walk to the *shamshan ghat,* as the pyre had to be lit before the sunset. Kunal was especially relieved when the journey ended. The body was set on the top of the pyre. Kunal's father handed him a burning log. Amid the chanting of the priest, Kunal placed the log and lit the pyre. He squinted his eyes as he watched the flames consume his mother's body.

Generous amount of oil and *ghee* were poured on to the flames, making the fire fiercer, so that the worldly chains that held the soul hostage, would melt away. As the mortal shell burnt into a charred, grey ash, the soul freed itself from earthly bonds to join the *Supreme Being in* heaven.

A mild breeze started blowing. A few glowing embers combined with the powdery ash and flew westward. As the breeze got stronger, the embers were carried into the sky, upwards. Slowly, they drifted further and further, until no human eye could see where they finally rested.

Now, his mother was truly gone.

Kunal turned his head away from everyone and *wept.*

The next few days were a very confused period for Kunal.

He started feeling guilty about playing God and taking his mother's life. His relatives were consoling him while his conscience screamed the word "*murderer*" into his ears, incessantly.

No one knew what he had done in the hospital.

He *dared* not admit it to anyone.

Their house was cluttered, dirty and in complete chaos. Kunal found it extremely disturbing to see that things were not in their place. There were shoes everywhere! Sleeping arrangements had to be made for all the relatives, and that meant the sofas had to be moved and folding beds had to be brought in from the storeroom. The bathrooms were a mess and the kitchen, a pile of dirty utensils. Everything was in disarray and he desperately wanted everything to be back to normal and orderly, just as it was when his mother was alive.

At times, felt so agitated that he felt that he could *kill someone!*

"Hadn't he already done that?" his conscience jeered at him, every now and then.

After the *havan* ceremony, performed with the purpose of granting eternal peace to the departed soul and for purifying the house, his relatives began to leave. They were sad and mournful as they left. Kunal, however, was happy that they were leaving. He had a spring in his step as the last distant aunt hugged and kissed him and left.

"At least the house will not be a mess anymore," he thought to himself.

Usually, after a big family event, his mother had the house return to normalcy within a single day. She could not rest until all the bed sheets and towels were washed, the floors mopped, and the folding beds put away. The bathrooms were cleaned with strong bleach, and the sofas were placed exactly where they belonged. The servants had to work hard that day!

Kunal, took upon himself to perform that task. He started taking the bed sheets off the makeshift beds, the towels out of all the bathrooms and instructed the servants to start washing. Then, he went to the kitchen and told the maid to wash all the dishes, as he cleaned the floor. He mopped and scrubbed tirelessly, until all the stains were gone, and the floors were spotless.

He arranged everything back in the shelves. He put fresh sheets on his mother's bed. He went to his room and removed all the clothes that belonged to Sushma auntie and put them in a large garbage bag. He told Kamla to have them thrown away. She stole looks at his father as she grabbed the bag and took it to the garbage dump outside the house. The servants worked hurriedly and helped in putting the large pieces of furniture where they belonged. Kunal went to his mother's temple room and lit an incense stick. He opened all the windows to air the house.

Soon, the house was starting to look like how he remembered it.

Only then, Kunal went to his room to shower and lay down. He slept fitfully until he was awakened by his father at dinner.

He came to the dining table and was happy to see a clean table with food neatly laid out. Kamla had made his favorite food, *stuffed aloo parathas*, and he ate slowly. The food tasted the same as before, but it was hard for him to swallow knowing that his mother was gone, *forever*.

His father watched him intently, even when Kunal was avoiding eye contact with him.

"So, how is school? Still in love with architecture or do you want to join my Chartered Accountancy firm?" he said jokingly.

Everyone knew how much Kunal hated accounting.

"No, Dad. Thank you. I am happy with my career choice and I have no desire to join your firm," Kunal said, smiling for the first time as if in years. *"Actually, I have a few friends who are planning to go to US once they finish their degree. I think I would like to do that as well."*

"*Oh, that is a little unfair. I will be completely alone. Why not start your own consulting firm in India? I will loan you the money and you can return it when you start becoming profitable,*"

Kunal's father offered.

"*No, thank you. I think that I need to get out of here for a little while and gain some experience before I start on my own.*"

"*I see. You have made up your mind, then. Here, eat some more chicken curry. You look extremely pale and tired. You must know that I am really sorry that you had to see your mother suffer for so long. I was hoping to bring your mother home for one last time,*" his father said in a low voice.

Kunal genuinely felt bad for his father for a moment.

CHAPTER

THIRTY TWO

I HAVE TOILED
IN THE SUN . . . 1955

Kunal's father, Anand Sinha, was not a billionaire. However, he had made a sizable fortune for himself and was one of the wealthiest persons in the city.

He had two offices in the heart of Mumbai. He employed about fifty people in each office and had proven to be a good, as all his original employees were still working for him.

A large number of Bollywood actors were his clients. He often had invitations to attend high society parties. He was considered one of the wealthiest people in Mumbai and was a much-respected member of the city's social circle.

Life had not always been this easy for Anand.

His mind often drifted to the year 1947, when India was granted freedom after a long period of oppressive British Rule.

In August of that year, the British had decided to mercilessly cut India up. India was divided into three parts: Pakistan, Bangladesh and India. What followed was, and is still, considered the saddest and bloodiest chapter in India's history. Hindus, who lived in the area now designated as *Pakistan*, had to migrate to mainland India. Many, but not all Muslims, had to leave India for Pakistan.

The exodus of a million people from Pakistan to mainland India and vice versa had left the society in turmoil. Hindus and Muslims were killing each other lawlessly. Extremely rich families had to leave all their belongings in Pakistan and migrate to mainland India. On their way across the *British made border*, hundreds of thousands of people were looted, raped and killed.

Violence broke out in the streets and there was senseless bloodshed, murder and chaos. Human life lost its dignity and meaning in the ugly spectacle of hatred and sheer madness. Hindus were killing Muslims and the Muslims were butchering the Hindus. Women were raped and children were terrorized and killed. There were horror stories of Muslims tossing Hindu babies in the air and catching them at their sword points, skewering them to their death.

Just making it alive through the border was a major achievement.

Refugees arrived in hordes, penniless, hungry and exhausted. They were housed in makeshift camps. Many died in the ordeal that followed, facing hunger, heat, starvation and poor living conditions.

Refugees stayed in the camps until arrangements could be made for them to travel to their relatives. Then, they had the formidable task of rebuilding their lives, literally starting from nothing.

Anand's father was living in the Pakistani part of Punjab when the news came of partition. In a frantic attempt to reach India, his father, Kedar Nath Sinha, had left his home and wealth in the small town named Bhawalpur. Anand was only twelve years old, when his father had hurriedly herded them to the train station in the middle of night and shoved them onto a train headed for India. They had left their house in the wake of mob fury and were not able to take any belongings with them. Anand's father had been tipped off by a Muslim friend that they should leave for India as soon as possible before things got too bad. They boarded the night train and escaped to India just in the nick of time.

Later, the trains that carried passengers from Pakistan arrived at the station dripping blood. All the passengers had been gruesomely murdered by the Muslims crazed and maddened with hate. Thousands of relatives came to the train station, only to see the murdered bodies of their loved ones and dead faces of their brothers, uncles and aunts. Invariably, the young women were raped or tortured. In many instances, they were killed, and their breasts were chopped off their bodies.

Anand's father had relatives in Bombay and that was their final destination. The train had only brought them as far as Amritsar. They still had to find transportation to Bombay.

At least they were able to reach India alive! Hundreds of thousands of people would not make it alive while crossing the border towards either side. Hindus and Muslims were killing each other as mob violence had taken over the entire country.

In the days that followed, Anand's father sold his gold watch. The money was still not enough to pay for their way to Bombay. Anand's mother's gold necklace was sold next. It was her *mangal sutra,* the symbol of a wedded woman that traditionally, was never removed as long as the woman stayed married. However, money was much needed, and it was not the time for considering sentiment or honoring lame, meaningless tradition.

Anand's father was able to buy tickets to go to New Delhi by bus. After arriving in New Delhi, they had to wait for three days at the railway station, to catch the next train to Bombay.

To this day, Anand could not remember the events from that time very clearly. Apparently, his mind had chosen to dull the gory memories of that horrendous journey.

Anand was the eldest of six children. Anand's father was a railway employee and had five sons and a daughter. He could barely pay for all the children's schooling. Even if he wanted, he could not have supported Anand's college education. He reminded his family repeatedly, to consider themselves lucky that they were alive and had a roof above their heads. College education was almost a luxury and at that time thoughts of luxuries could not even be entertained.

Anand had finished his high school and decided to look for a job to raise his tuition for college.

In the post-independence years, jobs were hard to come by. The country was still ravaged by the aftermath of the British rule and the Partition. Anand's first job was at the age of twenty years. He was hired to work as an ordinary peon in an office.

He lived like a pauper and saved all of his money that he humanly could. He enrolled in the cheapest college to take accounting classes in the evening after he finished work. It was very hard for him to make ends meet. He borrowed money from his relatives to buy a bicycle. He was deep in debt and had to work constantly; doing menial jobs, waiting tables, cleaning offices until his degree was complete.

His first job at a bank after three years of struggle, was a big event for him. During these years, he had borrowed money from so many of his friends that he felt embarrassed in their company. He worked hard at his job and continued to work on his second job. His initial salary was only Rs 700 Per month, and he owed Rs 4,000. He was so hell bent on being debt free that he spent every waking hour working. Slowly, but surely, he started paying off his debts, one by one.

He kept a meticulous journal and logged his expenses and earnings. It took him two full years to pay all his debts with interest. After paying off his debts, he started contributing towards his younger brothers and sister's education as well. His father's meager salary as a railway ticket collector did not go far and a little extra money was a big help.

Now that Anand was debt free, his parents started indicating that he should get married. Marriage in those days was routinely completely arranged by the family elders.

The bride and groom barely knew each other, prior to their marriage.

His aunt knew of a distant relative who knew of a girl from a good family from the same sub caste as theirs. She was insistent in her suggestions that Anand should go and see the girl. He knew that seeing the girl actually meant agreeing to marry her. He wanted to wait and collect more money, so that he could have a more secure beginning to his married life. Also, he was waiting to be promoted to the position of senior clerk of the bank. After the promotion, his plans were to seek a career in a private accounting firm. He did not want to get tied down by getting married at that point in his life.

A year later, on combing through the employment section of the newspaper, he saw a vacancy for an accountant at a small taxation and accounting firm. He sent in his application. The next few days were spent eagerly waiting for an interview. When Anand showed up for the interview, wearing his only suit, he was terrified to see that there were around twenty-five candidates in the waiting room. They were all there to interview for the same job!

Anand considered himself extremely lucky, when he received the appointment letter confirming the fact that he indeed had been hired!

In those days, good jobs were hard to come by. India had newly become independent and was still trying to become a republic. The constitution was being written, and laws were being formulated. The horrendous chapter of Partition was over, and India was awakening herself after a long slumber, slowly beginning her journey to pursue a path of progress and becoming a member among the nations of the world.

There was utter chaos, and the economy was completely in shambles.

Families were still trying to find means of making money. The desire to settle down and achieve financial security was foremost in the minds of young people entering the work force. However, the basic laws of society still held true; skills such as hard work and job proficiency and assets such as education were highly valued.

Anand's father made sure that all five children were enrolled in school. Anand, by virtue of being the oldest son was harnessed into the task of helping the family financially. He was happy to take on the responsibility and contributed money regularly towards his siblings' education.

Those were unusual and remarkable times. Ordinary people had sacrificed their lives for India's independence and sovereignty during the struggle for freedom from the British and had proven themselves to be heroes. Mahatma Gandhi was holding a fast until death unless Hindus and Muslims stopped senseless killing of each other.

In the midst of such lofty drama, Anand's contribution to his own family seemed miniscule in comparison.

CHAPTER
THIRTY THREE

WILL YOU MARRY ME . . . ?
1963

After two more years, when Anand's father suggested that it was time for him to get married, Anand readily agreed. He was debt free now and was on his way to saving himself a tidy sum of money.

A suitable girl was found with the help of his relatives. He was informed that he had to see a girl. Her name was Kanta. She was from a very good family, was beautiful and he would definitely like her. He was given a black and white picture of her and told that he should be ready to meet the girl on the coming Tuesday. All Anand could say was "sure".

Until now, Anand had been so busy taking care of his younger siblings' education and paying off his debts that he had not given the subject of marriage a great deal of thought. When he looked at the picture of his future wife, he was happy. She was truly beautiful.

He tapped into his savings for a brand-new suit and a good pair of shoes. He bought 2 shirts, 2 silk ties, one pair of cufflinks and two pairs of socks.

The day he was supposed to meet his future bride for the first time, he had a haircut and a professional shave. His younger brothers and sister laughed quietly at him as they saw him look at himself in the mirror repeatedly. He stared at them and told them to go to their room and read. He put on his new suit. His shoes had not been broken in and pinched at his toes. His shirt collar was over starched and too stiff. It took him a long time to figure out how he was supposed to wear a shirt with actual cuff links.

Finally, he was ready and thought that he looked fine. He took a deep breath and stepped out of the house along with his younger brother and his parents. His aunt, who was the designated matchmaker in the community, was going to join them at the bus station.

Kanta belonged to a very rich family. Her father was one of the leading entrepreneurs and owned multiple businesses in the city. Needless to say, their house was in a very posh area of the city. A taxicab was arranged to pick his family up from the bus station and drive them to their house. (It would have been too expensive to pay for the cab fare for the entire distance).

When Anand saw Kanta's house, he thought that someone must have made a mistake. The house that sprawled in front of his eyes was a mansion. The entrance had a large iron gate. A gateman was housed permanently to greet the visitors and escort them inside.

Anand was instantly belittled by the sight of the enormous house. Surely, his family did not measure up to this kind of wealth. He was a little disappointed and thought that the match was not going to materialize. As they went through a passageway lined by huge palm trees into the house, his brand-new suit appeared tasteless and vulgar to Anand. They were led to the drawing room, which was splendidly decorated with large paintings and beautiful furniture.

When he saw Kanta for the first time, Anand thought that he had never seen anyone as beautiful. She was clad in a sky-blue sari. She did not need any kajal or face powder and would have looked better without any makeup, he remembered thinking. Kanta came to greet his family wielding a tray in her hands which had six teacups and a tea kettle.

Indisputably, those were the best teacups he had ever seen!

Then she proceeded to say *"hello"* to him and *"namastay"* to his parents. The maidservant made tea, and Kanta handed the delicately patterned teacups to everyone present.

That was the best cup of tea he had ever had in all his life!

After that, she sat down and had politely answered all the questions his relatives shot at her. She made another trip to the kitchen and brought out another tray which had the most delicious biscuits he had ever tasted.

He wondered if he could find any fault with her at all!

Anand considered a married man's life to be more peaceful and desirable as compared to his current existence. Anand had met some of his friends' wives. They were loud, brash and very unladylike in comparison to Kanta. They argued with their husbands in loud and angry tones and addressed them by their first names. Anand preferred the traditional values of family life and was not comfortable with the notion of a modern woman as his future bride. Frankly, independent type of women, intimidated him a little.

He could not recall the conversation he had with Kanta. On his way back, he was already thinking of the kind of house he was going for his future family. He had already decided that he was going to have two children, and in his imagination his children looked exactly like Kanta.

When he reached home, there were numerous relatives waiting for him. He had to answer all of their questions. All of them wanted to know when the wedding was going to be held.

His mind was made up already. He really liked Kanta and wanted to marry her as soon as possible. If she could be his wife, he would be extremely happy. Rather, he would consider himself to be the most fortunate person in the whole world.

There was only one hiccup. A niggling thought crept into his mind and bothered him constantly.

Kanta's family was extremely rich. Her father was among the top wealthiest families in Bombay. Anand's family was barely managing to make ends meet.

Why would they want their only daughter to marry into his family? A possible alliance between the two families did not seem realistic, even in Anand's wildest flight of imagination.

As weeks passed and there was no further communication from Kanta's family regarding the *rishta*, Anand tried to forget about the entire matter and focus single mindedly on his career.

CHAPTER
THIRTY FOUR

RAGS TO RICHES . . .
1963 TO 1965

Luckily, his new job paid him more money than his job at the bank. His boss, Shri Narinder Sharma was highly impressed by his hard work. He called him one evening and asked him to meet him at his house.

Narinder Sir (as he used to address his boss) greeted him warmly and welcomed him to his house. As Anand sipped tea in his front lawn, he wondered why he was being so nice to him. After a few niceties, Narinder Sir came to the point.

"Look, Anand. I wanted to discuss a business idea with you. I know that you are very knowledgeable and that you also work hard. I think that your future can be extremely lucrative if we start a business together.

We can open our own firm. I will provide the finances and you can put together a team of people and run the company."

"Oh, really. You mean our own accounting firm? Wouldn't it make our current company owners upset? I am sure there will be a legal issue?"

"No, no. There should be no legal repercussions as long as we abide by the legal provisions in our contract to the letter. I will consult with a lawyer and we will go from there. All you have to do is keep a log of all the clients that you serve, so that we can contact them when we start on our own."

"So, that is what Narinder Sir wants!! He wants me to steal the existing clients from this company!" thought Anand horrified at the blatant dishonesty.

He wanted to help Anand sabotage the company that he was working for, rob their clients and then start their own venture. This was pure thievery, and Anand could not imagine stooping so low to get ahead in life. He could not be a part of it. The mere thought of doing something so unethical was repulsive to him.

"Well, we will split 60/40. You keep 40% of profit and I will bear the operating expense," Narinder Sir went on with his proposal.

Anand's mind performed some mental arithmetic, and he could imagine how much money there was to be made. He, however, had already made up his mind. He did not want to compromise his principles or do something dishonest.

"Narinder Sir ji. How about I think it over for a few days? I will let you know in a week or two."

He finished his tea, picked up his briefcase and slowly walked out of the house onto the crowded streets of Bombay.

He would never go along with this venture.

If he did anything, he would do it all on his own. He will not steal any clients. He will work hard, but he will keep *HUNDRED* % of the profit!

It was an important day for him, because from that day onwards he thought of nothing more than starting his own company. He believed that when the time was right, he would not have to look for clients. He intended to work hard and build a name for himself. Then he would have a company so great that there would be no dearth of clients. He visualized a waiting room full of people, waiting for consultation with *him*.

He had to figure out how to start his own company. He started this by doing what he normally did to achieve any target, big or small----by starting a new TO DO list!

He figured that he would need a lot of money to start his venture. The good thing was that he was debt free at this point. The bad thing was that he had no cash to speak of.

The first item on his list was to find out exactly how much money he needed.

The second item was location of his proposed office.

Third on the list was to have a legal document drawn up for his venture.

Fourth, he would need clients.

As he was not going to be unethical and steal clients from his current company, he had to factor in advertising expenses.

Fifth, a phone number and staff to help him run the business.

Sixth item was to hire a team. This was laughable as *he* was going to be the one-man team. He will answer his own phone, clean his own office and provide tax accounting solutions to his clients.

Anand realized that he had another *to do* list assigned to his marriage and he had not even started working on that!

All he could do was to work even harder at his job and continue to save whatever money he could.

CHAPTER

THIRTY FIVE

A MATCH MADE
IN HEAVEN . . . ? 1965

Anand's father and uncles, however, continued to derive immense pleasure from discussing the riches of Mr. Goswami. Often times, they enumerated his many business ventures and his total estimated wealth whenever they sat together. Anand listened to these discussions with a keen ear.

He could not help but think wistfully that with a little help from Kanta's father, he could easily turn his dreams to reality. What would take a lifetime for him to achieve, could be done very quickly, if he could get a little financial backing and a few contacts.

Slowly, he became extremely interested in discussions regarding Mr. Goswami's family and his riches. It surprised his family members, as earlier he had shunned all talk in this matter, stating that the Goswamis were way too rich as compared to their family and would never consider their alliance seriously.

His younger brothers and sister giggled at him as he asked more questions about Kanta's family. How many siblings did Kanta have? How many factories did they own? What was the possible value of their house and their cars?

"Why would Kanta ever agree to marry him? If she saw the poor two room house in which they lived she would be horrified, "Anand thought timidly.

Four of his younger brothers and one sister shared one room and the second room belonged to his parents. Anand slept on a makeshift bed in the kitchen after dinner.

If Kanta knew that they did not own a car, she would definitely not consider marrying him. The one sofa that they owned was ripping at the seams and the carpet had so many stains that it was embarrassing. As he looked around his house, the peeling paint and the signs of poverty jeered at him. The ceiling fans were probably thirty years old, they still cooked on a kerosene stove and his parents and brothers and sisters were dressed in clean but old clothes which could not be called fashionable by any sense of the word.

He took out his account book. He had a total of 5700/- rupees saved up so far. He started thinking about using that money for a facelift for his house. Property values in Bombay were too high to consider moving to another house. He decided to spend the money on fresh paint and a new sofa set. He bought a propane cooking range, brand new dinner plates and cutlery. He was also mindful of his brothers and sister's clothes and bought them a new outfit each. His father got a new suit, and his mother got a new sari. He instructed everyone not to wear their new clothes until he told them to.

The final purchase was a secondhand scooter.

Finally, all the items on his list were crossed out. His house started to appear presentable, but all his money that was saved with such hard work and frugality was gone! He also had a scooter to ride and did not have to take the bus everywhere. Life seemed to be moving forward.

Now, he felt ready to woo her.

Anand told his father to contact Kanta's family again to let them know that he was keen on going ahead with the alliance. He asked his father to invite Kanta's parents to their house for tea.

Kanta's father was not surprised to hear back from them. His flourishing textile business had ensured that there were many persistent suitors for his daughter. He, however, wanted to wait for the right person to come along. So far, he had seen a lot of young men who seemed more interested in his money than his daughter.

"It is better to wait," he thought sadly.

Anand seemed different from the other suitors. There was something about Anand that made Mr. Goswami genuinely like him. He liked that he was hardworking and brilliant. He was also impressed by the fact that Anand was well spoken.

Mr. Goswami did *not* like the fact that Anand had such a large family. The mere idea of his daughter having to take care of so many family members was not very palatable to him. He was aware that Anand's family was not wealthy. However, with God's grace, he had enough money to ensure that his daughter would always have a comfortable life.

He accepted Anand's invitation and sent a message that they would be happy to join them for tea.

This threw Anand into another bout of *making-a-list* frenzy.

Anand was extremely nervous about the upcoming tea party. With great deal of attention to detail, he created the menu for that night. The children were told to behave and greet their guests by saying *namastay*. They were instructed to smile all the time and talk as little as possible.

Also, proper eating etiquette was discussed. They were commanded to wear their best clothes and Anand's mother was told to put on makeup and her best jewelry. His father was sent for a fresh haircut. Everyone's shoes were polished and shined by the youngest brother. The new tea set was taken out and dinner napkins were laid out.

His youngest sister was overwhelmed by the activity in the house. She walked around the house in discomfort as her new clothes and shoes felt uncomfortable. Nevertheless, she could not take her eyes off her beautiful, shiny shoes.

Anand almost felt sorry for putting everyone through this debacle. His last surveying look at the house made him feel that it was all worth it. The house was clean, the floors were scrubbed, all the junk that his mother had hoarded for years was thrown out, the walls had been freshly painted and the food was laid out in beautiful new plates.

The evening went well as Anand was able to put Kanta's parents at ease with his good humor. They were visibly impressed by the kids' good behavior and the clean house. The youngsters ate their snacks with extremely good manners and left the grown-ups to talk. Anand cleared the dishes himself, solely because he was too worried about someone dropping the new plates and destroying the whole set.

He could see Kanta's father getting impressed by the display and he was secretly happy that his plan seemed to be working. He had played his cards right so far.

As soon as he could speak to Anand alone, he started asking the expected questions.

"So, Anand, how much do you get paid every month?"

"I get 1700/ rupees per month."

"Really!! That is a lot. How come you get paid so much?"

"Well, it is a little embarrassing, but I will tell you the truth. My actual job pays me Rs 800/ but I do some extra work on the side. I have done a lot of odd jobs so far. I have even worked in a restaurant waiting tables when the money was tight. Luckily, these days, I compile taxes for two businessmen on a monthly basis. That brings in some extra money. So, 1700/ is a combination of money from my job and the extra work. I am hoping that in a year or so, I can save money and start my own accounting firm. As you know, it is not easy to own an office in a city like Bombay. All commercial properties are extremely expensive."

Anand could see a smile creeping up on the old man's face. He thought that Mr. Goswami was laughing inwardly at his meager income. However, he held his head high and looked earnestly into his eyes.

"Why don't you come by my office tomorrow? Maybe, I can free up some space for you to start your own office."

'Oh, that will be perfect. What time would you like me to show up tomorrow?"

"Say, around 10 am."

"Thank you, sir. I will be there."

They shook hands and started to head out the door.

That was when Mr. Goswami realized that the whole evening had gone by without any mention of Kanta.

As he waited for his driver to bring his car around, he looked into Anand's eyes and said, *"Well, young man. How come we have not discussed Kanta? I assumed that you were going to express your interest in marrying my daughter. Was I wrong? Do you not want to marry her?"*

"Oh yes, I do. Very much so. But sir, here is the thing." Anand moved closer to Kanta's father and turned to look back at his small house.

He pointed towards it and said, *"Do you think that I will bring my bride to this place which is more a khaal than a house? I want you to give me a year. Let me run my own business for a year and then buy a real house for her to come to. If it is okay with you, we can get engaged now and get married next year. I will make sure that by then, I will have more money and can keep her comfortable."*

The old man broke out in a loud laugh and Anand was worried for a second. He waited with clenched fists for a long minute thinking that Mr. Goswami was going to insult him. Luckily for him, it turned out that he was merely laughing at his meticulous planning for the future. Mr. Goswami was still laughing and wheezing a little when he got into his car.

As he left, he patted Anand on his back and exclaimed, *"You are an unusual man. Meet me tomorrow at my office!"*

Anand was relieved at the end of the evening. As far as he was concerned, the evening had played out exactly as he had wanted, and he could not have asked for more. He took his brothers and sister to the nearby ice cream shop and bought them a treat for being so good.

Then he started to prepare for the next day.

Anand woke up bright and early, put on his good suit and shoes and took the bus to Santa Cruz where the head office for Goswami Textiles was located. The office was in a large building. The receptionist asked him to wait as Mr. Goswami was in an important meeting. She asked if Anand would like some coffee.

Anand declined and settled into a couch and picked up a magazine from the stack on the coffee table. He had to wait for about thirty minutes before Mr. Goswami showed up. He was dressed in a simple shirt and pants and took Anand to his office.

As he sat across the table, Anand realized how successful Mr. Goswami truly was. He employed a huge staff and was crisp in his orders to them. He did not seem to be a very patient or a tolerant person as his employees carried out his orders promptly.

His textile company was among the limited few that had ventured into polyester fabric before the competition caught on. Polyester had become the dream yarn with its indestructible, silky fabric and bright colors. It was relatively inexpensive as compared to silk and could easily be afforded by the poor. Young men were wearing shirts made of the fabric and women were adorned in polyester sarees anywhere you looked.

As the only major textile manufacturing unit in western India, Goswami Textiles was a hugely successful business venture. The company traded on the stock exchange and its stock price had risen steadily.

Anand felt belittled in the presence of this man who headed such a large business. The enormity of the moment made him a little sweaty in his palms.

"So, are you ready to see your future office?"

"Yes, of course."

"Follow me."

He walked through the narrow hallway and reached a small door that was locked. Mr. Goswami took out a key from his pocket and opened the door. As they walked in Anand was pleasantly surprised to see a very respectable wooden desk and a leather chair, very similar to the one in Mr. Goswami's own office. The room even had a window with a view looking into the street. There was a phone on the desk and a filing cabinet and Anand felt as if his dream was unfolding right in front of him.

"So, what do you think?"

"It is very nice, but I do not think I can afford it. The rent alone will be more than my current income."

"Yes, that is true. I was thinking of loaning it to you for a year and then later on you could consider it your wedding gift."

"It is extremely generous of you. I better accept your offer before you change your mind."

Anand shook hands with Mr. Goswami, rubbed his hands together and looked around at his future office.

"So, who are your current clients?"

"Well, I have only two so far. One of them is my friend who has a small garment shop in Bandra. The other one is a small restaurant in Worli, where I used to work. May I ask who your accountant is and how much do you pay them?"

"I honestly do not know, and I can have you meet with our general manager on Monday. He can show you the outline of our operation and how much money the accounting firm is charging us. Maybe you can help us with our taxes," Mr. Goswami said thoughtfully.

"That will be wonderful. I promise you that you will not regret this decision."

Mr. Goswami smiled at him again, however, the mirth in his eyes disappeared soon. He nodded mysteriously at some thoughts in his mind and Anand suspected that there was something that he did not want to share with him just yet.

WILL YOU TAKE CARE OF HER? JANUARY 1966

Marriage, in addition to his career, was on Anand's mind constantly. Sometimes, when he thought about all the things that he had to take care of and how much work it entailed, his mind started spinning.

The only way he could handle it was by making his *"to do"* list.

His family members jokingly teased him about his unending lists. For Anand, his list was a very helpful tool that kept him on track in his path of life. He frequently lectured his younger siblings about making a list of their tasks every day, to be successful in life.

His list got longer and longer.

The next few days were marked by the most wonderful bit of frenzy Anand had ever known in his life. His lists were endless, and he could barely cross out a few items and he had to add more.

He advertised for a secretary/receptionist and hired the first girl who called. He had the cheapest signboard that he could find to put outside his office. He transferred his textbooks into the office, printed out cheap stationery with his office name and logo on it.

He made handwritten pamphlets advertising for his office and left them in his friends' businesses, public places and even movie theater bathrooms. He relentlessly waited for the phone to ring.

He offered to give free tax advice to his receptionist and asked her if she knew anyone who needed their services.

Mr. Goswami had stated plainly that he wanted to wait before he let Anand take over accounting for his business. Needless to say, he was being careful and was closely watching Anand's every move.

Thirty days passed and not a single client called. Anand was tired and discouraged. He sat in the leather chair and wondered if quitting his job was a good idea. He was going broke and was tempted to dial his friend's number to ask for the job for waiting tables again.

Luckily, he had no rent but even the receptionist's salary was hard to manage without any income. He was becoming increasingly despondent with each passing day. Six weeks from the opening of his office, Seema, his receptionist, called him to the desk phone.

"I think we have a client," she whispered, smiling at him.

"Hello," he gasped into the phone. *"How may I help you?"*

"Is this Anand Sinha?" asked the voice at the other end.

"Yes, it is."

"I am Rajeev Prashar and I saw your advertisement in the newspaper for accounting services. I have a fertilizer company and my accountant recently passed away. Would you like to meet me at my office today at 3 pm?"

Anand rapidly noted down the address, called for a taxi and told Seema to wait for his call.

When he called back, it was to tell his receptionist that she now had a permanent job and a raise. He also warned her that they will have to work really hard. He had landed the Prashar account and had convinced them to make an advance payment of Rs 10,000!

This was a lot of money and he immediately transferred it to his savings account. He invested half of it in shares of Tata Steel.

The next two months were grueling hard work. Mr. Prashar's company's operations were complex as they had multiple offices. Anand, being the perfectionist that he was, spent double the time on everything. On a few nights he slept in the office. His tax papers were ready two days before the promised date.

Mr. Prashar was overjoyed to see his taxes filed in time. He was especially impressed by the color-coded typewritten documents that Anand provided with clear breakdown of expense and profit of each branch of his company. His old accountant was old school and had only provided handwritten copies in the past. He was never thorough and had caused him a lot of trouble with multiple audits from ITO.

He paid him the remaining Rs 20,000. Anand was on cloud nine. He was careful and again invested half his earnings right away.

As Mr. Prashar handed Anand his check, Anand shook his hand and said, *"Sir, if you are happy with my work why don't you give my card to some of your friends or fellow businessmen. I can use some more work."*

This was probably the best advertising that Anand had ever done as it really paid off. His phone started ringing and he gained more clients. Soon, he needed to hire more staff and that office space was too small for his company. He started looking for a more spacious office. When he found an appropriate space, Anand negotiated and bargained with the landlord until they reached a mutually agreeable price. Anand finally signed an agreement for a lease to own.

Mr. Goswami was surprised when Anand knocked at his office door and asked to speak to him. He told him that he was going to move out by the end of this month, and he wanted to thank him for the opportunity. He told him in detail about his success so far and told him that he was on the lookout for a small house.

Also, that day, Anand ceremoniously asked Mr. Goswami for Kanta's hand in marriage.

That was when Anand learnt the *whole truth.*

"So, you have done really well, haven't you? You really want to marry her, don't you? You have really thought about it and really truly want to marry her?"

Anand could only nod his head in fervent agreement at all these questions. He was confident that he was doing well now and was deserving of this alliance.

Mr. Goswami's questions continued on.

"So, let's say, if my daughter agrees to marry you, do you promise to take good care of her? Do you promise to see to her well-being and spare no efforts in making her feel that you respect her?"

"Well, that is the purpose of marriage, is it not? To care for your spouse in sickness or health, poverty or wealth?".

"Well, sir? Looks like you are still in doubt of my ability to take care of her. Believe me, I have enough money right now to buy a house and to give her the comforts you would want her to have. And do not forget, I have only just begun. My firm is doing well, and I am planning to work even harder in the coming years. I do not ever want to face the years of struggle that my family has been through. I know I will succeed. I am always going to be successful, because I will work hard, harder than anyone else. I will do everything the right way and protect my business and grow it steadily. I will be honest and follow the rules, and do the right thing, however hard that may be. That is the reason you should consider me to be the best match for your daughter," said Anand, finishing his last sentence rather fervently.

Anand was surprised at his own courage.

"Who was he in this big city? A city that could easily swallow his ambition and not even care to spit him out," Anand thought inwardly. Yet, he had spoken his heart out.

Mr. Goswami raised his hand to quieten him. He paced back and forth in the room for the next five minutes in silence. Then he finally spoke.

"I think that you should know the full truth. Kanta, is the apple of my eye. I truly adore her because she is my daughter. If I had my way, she would spend her entire life with us. I would not ever part with her and have her stay in the house that she was born in. However, it is childish of me to think that. In all practicality she should have been

married two years ago when she turned twenty. That is the age when most of the girls in our family get married. She is already twenty-two. Do you know why she is not married? Do you know why I want to have her live with us all the time?"

"But then, how would you know. You see, Anand, Kanta suffers from epilepsy. I have not told even my closest friends about this. Her disease has been big reason why I am worried about her."

"Do you even know what epilepsy is?"

He turned to look into Anand's eyes.

"Do you?"

CHAPTER

THIRTY SEVEN

ROCK AND A HARD
PLACE . . . 1966

O f course, Anand only *vaguely* knew what epilepsy was.

Anand had seen one of his relatives have a *mirgi** attack during a wedding in the family. It was a frightening sight at the time and the memory had stayed with him. He was only a child and he remembered his distant uncle shaking violently into unconsciousness, the women in the house sticking a spoon in his mouth, making him smell a shoe and then try to slap him out of the spell that the *devilish mata** had cast on him.

He remembered asking his mother about why it had happened. Her simple explanation was that it was *mata** (an evil spirit), that had possessed his soul and the shaking was the result of the internal fight of his soul with the evil spirit. Of course, it was not a medical explanation, but at the moment it had sufficed in curbing his curiosity.

He was surprised however to see the very same *uncle*, an hour later, walking around without any problem.

He remembered being a little terrified of that *uncle* since then.

Silently, he sank into the chair in front of him. His recent bravado and euphoria from his success, his hopes of launching into the future, his dream of becoming the celebrated son-in-law of a prestigious family; seemed to blur into a hazy vision of his bride-to-be shaking uncontrollably, fallen on the ground.

He looked at the table in front of him for a long time. Then, he shifted his gaze to his shoes which had been polished until they shone like a mirror! His shirt collar stiffened around his neck and his throat felt as parched as a sandpaper.

He gulped repeatedly, until he thought that he could speak.

Eventually Anand got up and shook Mr. Goswami's hand.

"Now, I understand your hesitation and your questions. If I were in your shoes, I would be very skeptical as well. I am going to ask your permission to let me discuss this with my family. I need some time to be able to fully understand the implications of this fact. I would like to meet with your daughter, but only when I am ready to marry her."

"I want to take the time to make myself fully prepared for this. If I am not the person that I think I am, and decide that I cannot go through with it, I will let you know. Then you can despise me all you want to."

"Either way, I will come back to meet you in two to three weeks. I know that it is not easy for you to share this fact about your daughter's medical condition. I thank you and respect you for that. I hope you can

honor my request to have some time to think about it seriously," Anand said each word carefully.

Mr. Goswami nodded seriously with a distant look in his eyes. Anand caught a glimpse of a tear building up behind his gold rimmed glasses.

Mr. Goswami quickly turned and left the office.

Anand thought of all his married friends. All their wives were healthy (that he knew of). They mainly looked after the cleaning, cooking, giving birth to children and raising them. All of them were housewives. He had not ever heard any of his friends discuss their wives' medical issues. This was very strange for him, to imagine himself with a wife who had a serious medical condition.

When he looked at his own parents, his mother had managed the entire household and took care of everything from daybreak till nightfall.

She woke up at five thirty every morning and started by lighting her lamp in the prayer room. After her bath, she sat in her temple and prayed silently, ringing her prayer bell occasionally. She lighted incense in front of the deities and then started her day; heading to the kitchen to prepare morning tea and breakfast for everyone.

She had the tiffin boxes ready for the children (all six of them), stuffing them into their school bags. The small army of fresh-faced children marched to the nearby school; their schoolbags weighing their tiny shoulders down.

All these tasks were carried out like clockwork, with military-like precision.

After the morning burst of activity came the next section of housework: cleaning the house, washing the clothes if it was a sunny day, as clothes had to be dried in the sun on the clothesline in the tiny backyard.

Then, she went to the kitchen again to start cooking lunch, which comprised of a daal, chapati and vegetables. On occasion, there was a fancy chutney or a dessert as a treat. The children changed out of their school uniforms, right after reaching home from school.

Each child was given a glass of hot milk along with two biscuits, every evening before they started their homework.

Then, his mother watched over them until they started their homework, admonishing them wickedly if they did not complete it in time for dinner.

After his father got home from work, he showered and had a cup of tea. *Then* it was time for dinner. Everyone was required to sit at the dining table and have the same food that had been cooked for lunch, except that the chapatis would be made fresh again.

After dinner, the kids helped clear the table and his mother did the dishes. After an hour or so was bedtime. Anand always stayed up later, mostly reading a book. He woke in the morning with his book half-open most of the time.

He smiled to himself remembering those days.

"Would his future wife be able to handle the duties and tasks as his mother had? Would she be able to shoulder the responsibility of raising a family?"

His forehead wrinkled into a doubtful frown.

Of course, he wanted to marry Kanta; that would be the right thing to do. However, he did not want to do so without weighing all the implications.

Hence a *list* was needed!

CHAPTER THIRTY EIGHT

THE LIST OF PROS AND CONS . . . APRIL 1966

SECTION ONE
CONS

The illness.

This was going to be the biggest factor against his marriage to Kanta. With God's grace he was healthy. He had to stay healthy and strong. He had to work hard and have enough money so that he could look after his parents. His younger brothers and sister also needed to go for higher studies and university education was not cheap. He was not sure that he could add another person to his current roster of individuals who were solely his responsibility.

The embarrassment.

Whatever anyone might say, epilepsy was just not a disease that could be kept private. Sooner or later, everyone would come to know about it. The social gossip machine would have a field day. He knew firsthand that his relatives were not the kindest examples of the human race. He did not think that he could cope with the ridicule they might want to inflict on him.

The effect on his children.

He was not sure whether this was a disease that was passed on to the children or not. He had to find out more about it.

Future handicap.

He might have to shoulder a bigger burden as the years go by. Of course, he could not really control the future.

SECTION TWO
PROS

Financial gain.

Everyone knew how rich the Goswamis were. Anand stood to gain a lot of substantial financial gain from the alliance. Surviving in Mumbai was not easy. Cost of living was extremely high and owning a decent house was a dream that even very well to do people could not fulfil. Anand was sure that Mr. Goswami would help him immensely, monetarily. Even without asking, his father-in-law had been hinting at buying a house and a car for them as a wedding gift. Whichever way Anand looked at it, the house and a car seemed to be the honey that sweetened this deal beyond any criticism that could be leveled against it.

Anand felt a little sickened at his greed, initially. After a few days, he managed to convince himself that he should not look a gift horse in the mouth. If his father-in-law was hell bent on providing him riches in exchange for marrying his daughter with a medical condition, he would definitely not refuse them!

Doing the right thing factor.

Sort of self-explanatory. He would definitely feel that he was doing the honorable thing.

He would be revered by the Goswami family.

Cost of treatment.

He was sure that the treatment would be an added expense. He needed to find out more about that.

Course of illness.

The first thing he wanted to do was to meet with Kanta's treating doctor and understand the true nature of the disease. He needed to know the treatment options. Also, he needed to know how the disease was going to progress in future.

A mental picture about his future was forming in his mind now and he could see himself a married man. He could imagine himself reaching a step closer to his goal.

The family structure was changing, and people were having no more than two children: either by choice or by legislation. The dark period in Indian history was unfolding in front of his eyes as Indian prime minister had imposed "Emergency."

Mandatory vasectomies were inflicted on young men in an attempt to control the country's population. He would *definitely* not have five children like his parents! The government wouldn't allow it!

Yes, the family structure was changing.

He was planning to live in a house separate from his parents. His parents were still active and could take care of his siblings. He would definitely support them financially to help with their finances. This meant that the amount of work his future bride had to do was going to be much less than what his mother did. With the help of a maid, he could probably have his wife not have to physically exert herself as much.

Yes, it truly was possible. He could easily envision his future with Kanta.

He was a little embarrassed by his *list* making compulsion. Looking at his neatly written pages with perfect margins, he felt that he was cruel and heartless. Yet, it helped clarify some points in his head and simplified his decision.

He picked up the telephone to call Mr. Goswami. Then he thought the better of it and decided to visit him in person.

CHAPTER
THIRTY NINE

I WILL TAKE CARE OF HER . . .
JULY 1966

Anand had thought hard about the pros and cons of marrying Kanta. He knew that this was, by far, the most important decision of his life.

He was unable to forget the look of resignation in Kanta's father's proud eyes. However hard he tried to wipe that image from his memory, it kept on resurfacing in front of Anand's eyes.

He really did not want his decision about his marriage to be based on sympathy. He wanted to be objective, but his conscience had a constant murmuring monologue which told him that if he did not go through with it, he would lower himself as a human being. He felt morally bound to be a bigger person.

Maybe, it was because he had always been a caretaker for everyone and was a good human being.

Maybe, he was selfish and knew that Mr. Goswami was rolling in riches and could provide him a substantial advantage.

Maybe, it was just fate that compelled him to accept Kanta's hand in marriage.

Whatever the true reason, it felt right for Anand to marry Kanta.

The next morning, he told his parents to inform his matchmaker relatives, aunts, uncles to stop looking. He told them that he had decided about who he was going to marry.

His decision shocked a few, delighted a few and the remainder just felt sad that their services were no longer required. They started thinking of other single men and women that they could unite in holy matrimony.

He let his parents know that Kanta was the girl that he was going to marry. He also told them about Kanta's illness and that he was going to live in a different house as soon as they were married.

His parents were much in awe of their son who had worked so hard and brought the entire family out of poor financial conditions. They readily agreed with his decision.

His mother blessed him profusely saying *"Whatever you decide, son."*

His father muttered repeatedly, *"Very well, son. Very well, then. Very well."*

He vowed inwardly that he will adjust and do his best to take care of his future wife. He was not an absolute believer in *karma,* but the thought entered his mind that if he took care of Kanta, his own sister might find a kind soul who will take good care of her as well!

The very next morning, he made an appointment to meet Mr. Goswami and inform him of his decision.

He saw a look of relief in his future father in law's eyes.

Much in the manner of speaking as Anand's father, Mr. Goswami smiled briefly and muttered repeatedly, *"Very well, son. Very well, then. Very well."*

CHAPTER FORTY

KANTA . . . SEPTEMBER 1966

Kanta felt as if she had woken up in a half-dream. Her father had just told her that she was going to be engaged to Anand Sinha and will be getting married within the year.

She was going to have a husband, after all!

So far, getting married was considered an impossibility for Kanta. She had been prepared by her family members for the possibility of *never* becoming a bride, because of her *disease*.

Although she tried to hide it, the constant discussion of her *disease* had slowly eaten away at her heart. When she was little, she could not fully understand it. When she looked at herself in the mirror, she saw a normal person. After an *"attack"* she found herself surrounded by screaming family members in a panic. She could smell her vomit on herself and hated how helpless she felt. She just could not understand how the evil *disease* had possessed her. All the doctors that she was taken to for treatment, all the medicine she took, did not take her *disease* away.

The first time she remembered having an *attack* was when she was seven. The chauffeur was driving her back from school and was horrified to find her shaking uncontrollably in the back seat. He had driven home and ran inside the house to get her parents. By the time they came to the car she had stopped shaking but was covered in her vomit and had urinated on herself.

Her poor mother had never seen something like this, and immediately thought that this was the result of a curse placed on their family. Some wrongdoing must have been committed on their part and had invoked the wrath of God. She started chanting a prayer to her favorite god, *Shankar.*

Her father was the rational one. He drove her straight to the hospital and called his physician friend, Dr Bhaskar. He diagnosed Kanta with epilepsy and started her on a medication called Phenytoin that she had taken religiously, every day, without missing a single dose.

Her childhood was plagued by her *disease*. She cried impetuously at the limitations it placed on her life. Her parents did not let her out of their sight at all. She was not allowed to play with other children in the playground. She was not allowed to go to her friends' houses for birthday parties.

She felt conscious of the hooded eyes of her neighbors: mostly ignorant women, who whispered behind her back. She knew some of them believed that she *was possessed by an evil soul* during her attacks; that *another person's spirit* entered into her body. They believed that the seizure was due to the fight between the *spirit trying to own her body* and her *body trying to get rid of it*.

It was infuriating and frustrating for Kanta to try and dispel the fantastic notion conjured up by ignorant people. They preferred to cling to their own explanation, even though it was completely inaccurate.

The fact that she could not really have any friends was what really hurt. First of all, no one wanted to be her friend. Her schoolmates had seen her *attacks* twice by the age of ten. They were curious and a little scared of her. Even when they played together at school, they stared at her in awe. They never got too close, and kept a visible distance between them, *just in case*. It was clear that they did not want to be near her if she had that spell again. They definitely did not want to play at her house or invite her to theirs.

Needless to say, Kanta only had her maids or the maids' children for playmates during her growing years.

She was forever thankful to God for her father. He was an educated man who believed in science and would not hear of her mother's rants about evil spirits and black magic. He was a logical man who trusted medical science. He was diligent in providing Kanta the best possible treatment by the best qualified medical professionals that he could arrange for.

He laughed whenever Kanta's mother or his relatives brought forth the news of a saint or a priest who might help Kanta. They quoted examples of how a *sadhu* in a faraway *ashram* was known to drive evil spirits out of girls who had similar problems as Kanta.

One day, her mother's sister arrived with news of another quack. By this time, her father's patience had reached its limit and it was obvious that he did not want to hear another word in this matter. That day would be etched in her memory forever, as she had never seen her father so angry ever before. He stood up slowly from his chair, his finger pointed at her aunt, almost shaking in anger.

He spoke slowly, enunciating and emphasizing each word loudly for all to hear.

"If you talk about Kanta or her illness one more time, mark my words, one more time, you will have hell to pay. Remember, I will throw you out of my house if you ever talk about it again."

After these words, he stormed out of the house.

Her aunt had cursed aloud and cried and invoked the mercy of gods upon that house. Eventually, Kanta's mother told her to leave and implored her to never talk about Kanta's disease anymore.

Kanta had grown up thinking of herself to be a great burden on others. She knew that her parents sometimes felt ashamed of her disease. In spite of her father's attempts to shield her feeling inadequate in any way, as compared to other children, she considered herself unwanted. It did not help that her two younger brothers were healthy, and in the male dominated Indian society they were the darlings of all her aunts and clearly the most favored grandchildren. They were treated differently, with a lot more affection as compared to her. After all, they were the future heirs to the Goswami fortune.

Slowly, as she got older, Kanta came to terms with her place in the family.

Also, thanks to her father, she was encouraged to pursue her education. She developed a love for literature as it transported her to a faraway place, away from her home, *away from her disease.* As a lot of time was spent studying rather than being with friends, Kanta was a good scholar and always was at the top of her class in exams.

So it was, until the end of her twelfth grade. That was the year that changed Kanta's life forever, for worse. Kanta became extremely sick and developed a high fever along with cough. She had to be hospitalized with severe pneumonia. The fever was so high that she had multiple seizures every day. She had to be placed on very strong sedatives and was unconscious for a whole week. When she finally woke up, she was in a daze. She was weak and her memory was affected deeply from the multiple seizures.

Her mind would never be the same again. She did not admit to anyone, but she found it hard to remember simple facts. Her medication was increased even more, and she slowly experienced a period of seizure free interval. The medications however, made her feel nauseated all the time. Her doctor told her that she would get used to the side effects from the new medications slowly.

She started her Baccalaureate in literature and found it hard for her to excel at her studies. Her memory was not as sharp as before and she found it hard to concentrate. She could not keep up with the amount of studying required to pass her course. She was frustrated and fell into a deep depression. She stayed in her room and tried to read but it became harder and harder.

Finally, she gave up.

She informed her father that she would never be able to finish her degree. Her concerned father knew how much literature meant to her. He hired her a tutor who practiced reading and writing with Kanta every day. He also encouraged her to take music lessons as she was drawn to music. She had a sweet voice and soon learnt simple religious songs that the entire family was surprised to hear. She became the unofficial *bhajan singer* of the family during the religious ceremonies.

She was twenty-one years old now. Her parents were having frantic discussions regarding her marriage. Her father was skeptical about finding a match for her. There were many suitors and many families approached her parents seeking her hand in matrimony. However, as soon as her medical condition was divulged, there was a distinct lack of interest from the groom's family.

Kanta was not sure why her parents wanted to marry her off. She felt that she would never be comfortable anywhere else, except at her parents' home.

At least she was well cared for, here.

Who knew what kind of family she could marry into?

She had heard horror stories regarding mothers' in law and was extremely anxious about the concept of marriage.

Her aunts and her mother were obsessed with finding her a husband. They had turned on their matrimonial search engines and had contacted a reasonable number of business families for a suitable match. These families had a suitable boy, had heard of Kanta's father's wealth and were interested largely in a big, fat dowry. She went through the ritual of getting ready and bringing out the tea tray holding the dainty tea service, while smiling sweetly at all those present in the room. As if mechanically, she made useless conversation with the curious faces who looked up at her, *from the boy's side.*

They were obviously impressed by her beauty. The same admiring faces were instantly converted into apprehensive and shocked faces, the moment the family members were informed about her disease. This was then followed by a very polite yet hurried exit.

She had started playing a mental game where she would predict the time it would take for a certain family to leave after they were told the truth. Her *estimated time- to-exit* numbers were becoming more accurate lately.

The day her father told her about Anand, she was a little surprised. She had secretly observed Anand on a few occasions that he had visited the house to meet with her father. She instinctively felt that he was a good man. It did not seem as if he belonged to a big business family. Her father did not enumerate his business description, as he would normally do with other suitors.

Also, when she met his family members, *(with the beautiful tea-tray in her hand!),* she was able to tell that they were not rich. It was easy to see that everyone was a little uncomfortable in their brand-new clothes. They were polite though, and somehow her father did not mention her illness to this family. She was relieved and felt happy about that.

Kanta had finished her BA in literature, just a month before her wedding and was rather happy to be getting married. Now, she did not have to be the target of her relatives' questioning eyes, anymore; eyes that were filled with pity mixed with contempt underneath the cover of ever so present concern for her.

She did not feel the usual anxiety that new brides felt regarding their future. Her illness had made her appreciate the importance of being thankful for whatever had come her way.

Lately, she had started visiting her nearby temple on a daily basis. She had never been a religious person before, but now, she spent an hour in prayer at the temple. She had memorized and had started singing the holy songs of prayer, reciting the scripture, without fail every single day.

Maybe, it was the newfound faith in God that made her feel strong and at peace. She was not nervous when she took the seven circles around the fire with Anand in tow, in front of what seemed like a thousand people that had attended her wedding ceremony.

In her mind, Kanta was determined to be the best wife that she could be.

CHAPTER
FORTY ONE

MANGALAM VIVAH KARYA
(THE HOLY WEDDING)
NOVEMBER 1966

The month before the wedding was quite a blur for Anand. He was caught in a flurry of activity for the wedding. He had wanted a small wedding but his father-in-law had a huge family. He told Anand that he had immense business and family pressure to have a grand wedding.

He told Anand in no uncertain words, *"You might as well resign yourself to it, son. It is going to be a huge occasion. My favorite child is getting married! My wife and all the ladies in the house are **absolutely** going to run the show. My advice to you is this: Just go with the flow."*

In the next few weeks, Anand started to wonder if he was going to survive his own wedding. He felt that he was being engulfed by the buzz of activity. Days and weeks of pure confusion were colored with panic generated by all-knowing elder women of the clan. They frequently claimed that nothing was being done according to the mandatory customs.

Anand's mother squeezed the last bit of money out of him. It was being spent on what Anand considered useless things: jewelry and clothes for the relatives, new shoes and suits for his brothers, who were growing like weeds and their older clothes were now too small for them.

Anand's father dragged him to meet with the family priest. The priest was a true businessman and possessed well-honed skills to generate the most money from auspicious occasions. He quoted some *mumbo jumbo* from religious texts and successfully made them believe that God's blessings bestowed upon the newlywed couple would be directly proportional to the money that was paid to him.

The fact that his father-in-law was the one who did most of the spending, made it easy for Anand to be a willing participant in the event.

The wedding day finally arrived. Most certainly, it was the largest wedding that his immediate family had ever been a part of.

Anand was put through all the week-long rituals of Hindu wedding which culminated with seven circles around the fire at a certain auspicious time of the night (as determined by the priest based on the alignment of the stars).

He was exhausted when the wedding was finally over.

It was a proud moment for him when he brought his bride to his small but independent two-bedroom apartment that he had spent almost all his material wealth on. To Anand, his future home appeared miniscule as compared to the giant mansion that Kanta had lived in before that day.

Kanta brought many riches as her dowry when she became Anand's wife, thanks to her rich father. She was gifted a car and a driver as well as a fulltime maid who accompanied her from her father's house.

Anand couldn't be happier. He was happy with his new bride, happy to start a new phase of his life.

Over the next two years, he had started to admire Kanta. She was from a very rich family, but she did not spend money unnecessarily. She lived within her means and always managed to save money, a quality that Anand found very endearing.

Anand worked hard, spending long hours at work. His efforts started to pay off and he continued to get new clients. In a city like Mumbai, which was teeming with businessmen, there was no dearth of work. He was honest and extremely hard working. He *always* finished his clients' tax returns on time.

Soon, word about his firm started to spread and money started to pour in.

Anand occasionally worried about Kanta's disease. However, as luck would have it, she did not have any seizures.

Slowly, Kanta's illness was all but forgotten.

Finally, in the third year of their marriage, she became pregnant. Anand was overjoyed to hear the news.

The doctor wanted Kanta to be on different medication during the pregnancy for the safety of the fetus. Her pregnancy was progressing well *until* the sixth month, when, she had a full-blown seizure. The nightmare that Anand had forgotten, came back to haunt him again. He remembered feeling defeated that night and every following night of his life.

Luckily, Kunal was born without any complications. Kanta's only question to the doctor in the delivery room was to ask if the child was having a seizure. The doctor had repeatedly assured her that her baby was normal. Only time would tell whether the baby would develop epilepsy or not.

Anand was quick to have his son evaluated by an eminent neurologist who assured him that his son was not showing any signs of epilepsy. In spite of the neurologist's assurance that Kunal was free of epilepsy, Anand and Kanta still worried for Kunal.

At times, Anand saw Kanta looking at her baby and silently murmuring a prayer. Anand could read her thoughts and knew that she felt guilty that she may have passed on the disease to Kunal.

Anand reassured her time and again that there were no signs of epilepsy in Kunal and that according to the doctor Kunal was healthy. Anand's words did not do much to allay Kanta's fears. Sometimes, his own apprehension about Kunal's health was hard to hide behind his hollow words of encouragement. Even though he tried to soothe her worrying mind, the prospect of having passed on the disease to her baby and the accompanying worry made Kanta's eyes visibly tear up on numerous occasions.

CHAPTER

FORTY TWO

THE APPLE
OF MY EYE . . . 1968

Anand's joy knew no bounds!

Suddenly, there was a new purpose to his life now. Life was more and more worth living. Kunal quickly became the center of his existence.

According to Anand, there was no other newborn who was more beautiful than Kunal and he openly said so. Whenever he looked at Kunal's tiny little face he was overcome by pride and absolute joy. Anand had never in his life imagined that becoming a father would change his life so much. He was still busy at work and had to put in long hours, but his focus now was to rush home as soon as he could.

A few times, he asked Kanta and the maid to bring Kunal to his office just so that he could see him. Everyone thought that he was losing his mind over his child. Anand, however, could not care less.

Yes, he was happy with Kunal: his astonishingly remarkable and wonderful child who had already brought him every possible joy in the whole universe. He treasured every moment with him and was not ashamed to show it either!

His relatives were already hinting at more children, "*At least a jodi of boys- just like Ram and Lakshman,*" they suggested wisely. He smiled and dismissed them by a shake of his head.

Anand and Kanta had decided not to have any more children. The prospect of having a child with epilepsy was too harsh for Kanta to bear. Additionally, Anand did not want to ever risk Kanta having another seizure during pregnancy. She had suffered from a minor convulsion during pregnancy at twenty-two weeks. He had spent the whole night awake, worrying for Kanta and the baby's health. He was relieved to find out that it was *a fairly minor incident* and had not affected *the mother or the baby* (as the doctor put it). He did not want to relive that nightmare ever again.

Anand had already called the principal of the best school in the city to enroll Kunal. The principal had laughed loudly when he heard that the child in question was only six months old. Anand understood that he was going overboard with his plans for Kunal but only the best would do as far as his child was concerned. He constantly thanked God that he had the means to be able to offer his son the best of everything.

Anand's accounting firm was doing well, and he had branched out into two more offices; one in Santa Cruz and another in Andheri. He had hired four senior associates to run those offices. He was still very diligent and insisted on supervising all the major financial dealings himself, constantly making sure that everything was done right, and all the rules were followed to the letter. He had worked hard for an impeccable reputation in his business and wanted to continue to maintain a high standard. He did not want to be complacent and more importantly, did not want any mistakes that could tarnish his image. He wanted to be even more productive financially, now that he had a son and one day, hopefully, he would proudly pass his legacy on to him (much in contrast to what he had bequeathed from his own father: practically nothing).

Anand's father-in-law had become weak and frail and was homebound due to severe arthritis. He lived with Kanta's oldest brother as Kanta's mother had recently passed away from a severe bout of pneumonia.

Anand had taken care of his siblings; made sure that they went to college for higher studies and attained professional degrees. He had singlehandedly shouldered their educational expenses. They were good at studies and were able to land good jobs in their respective fields.

His younger brother, Manoj, had finished his graduate studies in Economics and Anand had hired him into his firm as a manager at one of the newer offices. His youngest brother, Rajesh, wanted to study Pharmacology. Anand had wanted him to study Accounting and join his firm as well, but Rajesh had no inclination or aptitude for Mathematics. His sister, Pratima, who was the youngest in the family and had just finished high school. She wanted to do pursue a career in Psychology and eventually wanted to teach at the University. He was very supportive of her studies and everyone could see that he was extra careful about encouraging her in her endeavors.

By the time Kunal was five years old, everything seemed to fall into place. Anand's brothers were also getting settled in life. They had completed their studies and were looking for their first jobs and were looking for their life partners to settle down and start their own families.

Pratima, however, had shown no interest in marriage and wanted to study for her Postgraduate studies before getting married. Anand had a long discussion with her. Indian society was just not ready for single women, he pointed to her. He placed a matrimonial advertisement in the newspaper, much against her will. He was able to persuade her to meet with a few young men who were suggested by one of the matchmaker aunts in their family. Eventually she agreed to get married, with extreme reluctance, warning Anand that she will continue to work towards her post-graduation in Psychology.

Anand had turned forty by the time all his responsibilities were taken care of. Now, his biggest joy was to watch Kunal grow. Just like Kanta, he worried about Kunal's health constantly. Lately, he had started to pray more than usual, asking God for blessing Kunal with a long healthy life and good fortune.

Kunal was growing fast. Every day, when Anand returned from work, he found new changes in him. All of his milestones were celebrated. Kunal's first tooth brought boxes of sweets to each member of his office staff. His first word was again a great achievement and was highly praised. When he took his first step, a few days before his first birthday, it was as if a miracle had taken place. All the servants in the house received a fat bonus on Kunal's first birthday. When Kunal went to his first day of school, time stood still for Anand and Kanta for a few hours until his return in the afternoon.

After Kunal's school started time took on wings and flew. Many a time, Anand and Kanta had turned to each other and wondered aloud at how rapidly time was passing and how quickly Kunal was growing. Kunal was turning into a strong and well-behaved child. He was brilliant at his studies. He played cricket in the school team. His Mathematics teacher always gave him more challenging questions to tackle as compared to the rest of the class. This fact brought extra happiness to Anand as he dreamt that one day Kunal would take over his firm.

Kanta, however, was deteriorating as far as her health was concerned. She had started having violent spells of seizures. In spite of the best treatment, her medical condition had started to worsen. She had more frequent attacks that left her unconscious for a greater length of time with each episode. She had now started losing control of her bowels and bladder during these seizures. Needless to say, the entire household was always on watch for these attacks as she needed to be hospitalized often. Their maid was in constant attention of her.

Anand was working long hours at work and his business was doing better than ever before. Instead of feeling happy and satisfied with his progress, Anand felt trapped and felt suffocated due to Kanta's illness. He did not visit any of his friends as he was tired of having to explain why his wife could not accompany him. He found it embarrassing that he had to constantly make excuses for her absence.

Only, Kunal brought him unbounded happiness.

One evening Anand came home and called out for Kunal. He was told that he had gone to watch a cricket match at the stadium with his friends. This piece of information shocked Anand.

"Was Kunal that old already?"

Kunal was fifteen years old now.

He had his own friends now.

The house seemed hollow without Kunal. Anand checked on Kanta, who was reading her favorite magazine and appeared to find his surprise amusing. The maid was laughing openly as Anand repeatedly said, *"itna bara ho gayaa? Kaise itna bara ho gaya, ekdum se?"*

He felt as if the walls of his house were closing in on him and he was restless. He waited for Kunal's return and it was only after he saw his face that he felt that he could breathe again. That day, he realized that he needed something more in his life.

Kunal will grow up and leave him someday; he shuddered inwardly at that prospect.

CHAPTER
FORTY THREE

THE DEVIL
IN THE SOUL . . . 1980

Anand's life had become monotonous. Especially, during the sweltering heat of summer, he found his daily routine depressing. The days were longer than usual, and business was slow. Most of his associates took time off to go on a vacation as children's schools were closed for a month and a half. Many of his friends were traveling with their families during the hot summer, as well. It did not help to hear them recount their tales of fun filled visits to different parts of the world upon their return.

Anand had always dreamed of traveling the world. Even though his financial situation had improved every year and they could afford to travel in luxury, Kanta's illness had kept them home bound. The thought of Kanta relapsing into her seizures while they were in a strange place, was a big deterrent to making any plans. Knowing that they could not travel, like everyone else made him frustrated and unhappy.

He felt that he had to do something different from his usual routine. Every now and then, he was overcome by the feeling of taking a break from his schedule and do something radically different, just for a change. At such times, he felt stifled and shackled to his constricted home life.

It had been a really good year for his business and in the year 1975 and his office staff was hinting at a party to celebrate the success. After a great amount of cajoling from his secretary, he gave in and also decided to attend. This was a big change for him. He used to hate the thought of going to social occasions. Now, he thought that if nothing else, it would be a change from his daily routine.

It was the evening of the office party that he met Sushma. She was a senior secretary at the city IT (Income Tax) office. His office staff had frequent dealings with her on behalf of multiple clients and everyone knew her very well.

She was also a very attractive lady who was recently widowed.

He could not take his eyes off her during the entire evening. He was very upset with himself as he considered himself to be a loyal husband and above all a gentleman. However, there was something riveting about how she conducted herself, talking to everyone at the party, chatting and laughing freely.

He was literally staring at her, when she turned towards him and introduced herself.

"Hello, I am Sushma."

"Oh, nice to meet you. I am Anand Goswami"

They shook hands and he felt uncomfortable right away.

She talked to him about politics and the latest tax laws and all he could come up with was to speak to her in monosyllables. He was struck by how alive and well informed she was. He found himself comparing her to Kanta and immediately felt guilty. He was tremendously angry at himself for doing that.

"So, where is your better half?" she asked him.

"Oh, she could not be here. She does not keep well and has been sick for a long time. She suffers from epilepsy," he told her.

He was really surprised at himself. Normally he would have lied and made some excuse for why Kanta could not be there that night. He rarely shared the details of Kanta's illness with anyone.

By the time he reached home that night, he found himself thinking of Sushma. There was something about her vibrant personality that he found extremely riveting. He found out where she worked. He had a lot of dealings with that office: mostly in the form of routine paperwork and submission of forms related to his clients' tax returns.

Normally his assistants carried out such tasks. Now, Anand went to her office on one pretext or another.

He knew that he was making it very obvious and that his office staff knew the real reason for his frequent visits to the Income Tax office, but the truth was that he could not help it. He *had* to meet her every now and then and find a reason to *speak* to her. It was almost as thrilling as a teenager's infatuation. In his heart, he did not consider himself capable of having an affair or disrespecting his wife or family. Yet, he could not stop himself from meeting her albeit under the cleverly devised pretext of *"office work"*.

He thought of her often. She was not even beautiful in the classic sense of the word. She was darker than most women, even Kanta. Every time he compared her to Kanta, guilt coiled inside him like a serpent ready to spring and poison his soul.

For a long time, it was enough for him to just walk by her, say the shortest sentence to her, sometimes simply steal a look at her without even her knowing that he was there.

She was, as he soon learnt, a very independent woman. She was recently widowed and had no children. Her husband died of a long and devastating illness a year ago. The gossip had it that she had a nervous breakdown after his death. Her mother and her sister had stayed with her for a year and had helped her back onto her feet. Now she worked full time. It was said that there was no need for her to work as her husband had left her a lot of money. She wanted to work mainly to fight living alone at home.

She was also an *alcoholic*. Surprisingly, everyone knew about her drinking. Anand found that hard to believe and blocked that piece of information out of his mind.

Anand was very moved by her story and wondered about her husband. Her bout of depression after his death made him think that she must have really loved him.

He was confused by how his mind was totally consumed by Sushma. At multiple times, he had indulged in his *list making habit* about Sushma, as well. The *pros and cons exercise* was worthless really, as all it did was drag him into thinking of her further.

There were days when Anand truly wanted his mind to be rid of Sushma. Especially now: his sick wife was worsening physically and trips to the hospital were becoming more frequent.

He tended to Kanta, accompanied her to the hospital when he needed to, enjoyed seeing her return to normalcy in between her spells. He felt relieved to hear the sound of her singing the bhajans in the morning, along with the ringing of the little bell in the temple.

*"But did he really **see** her beyond her incapacitating illness? Had he failed in keeping the promise that he had given to Kanta's father?"*

Soon, he stopped asking himself this question. He knew that he would go mad if he kept on analyzing and accusing himself.

He could see how happy Kunal was to see Kanta healthy and normal. He laughed more and held on to her hand and followed her everywhere in the house. It was a magical connection that he had with his mother. Kanta's health seemed to lend its vitality and happiness to Kunal as well.

However, the brief escape from the disease was broken frequently by yet another seizure, progressing into a relapse requiring hospitalization once again. The last few episodes of convulsions were so violent that Kanta had hurt her head on the edge of the headboard and the sight of blood on her clothes had terrified Anand.

Kunal became quieter after every spell of Kanta's illness. Often, Anand wondered what was going on in his son's mind. He tried to talk to Kunal about Kanta's illness, but the conversation always ended with Kunal blurting rudely, *"Yes dad, I know all that."*

Anand tried to keep Kunal engaged in his studies. The teenage years had built a wall between the father and son and each passing day it became more impenetrable. Slowly, Anand stopped trying as hard, decided to give Kunal more space.

He noticed that Kunal resented him, as if blaming him for his mother's illness. Other than heaving a deep sigh, Anand decided that he, really, could not do much to fix the situation.

CHAPTER FORTY FOUR

THERE GOES
THE SUN . . . 1985

In April, it was time for Kunal to leave home and head on to New Delhi to join Delhi Architectural College. To Anand, it seemed all too soon.

Was it not just yesterday that he was born? Anand could still see Kunal running around in the house chasing his friends, forgetting homework to play cricket (like all boys do!), demanding to buy his first bicycle at five years of age, that had to be bright red in color?

It seemed as if an entire age had passed within the blink of an eye.

Anand had wanted Kunal to become an accountant and join his company. However, Kunal had let him know, in no uncertain terms, that he would never be an accountant. With great passion in his youthful voice, he had explained to Anand that he was only interested in pursuing a career in Architecture.

Also, and this was truly heartbreaking for Anand, he did not want to go to college in Bombay. He wanted to go to New Delhi to join the DAC- Delhi Architectural College. As Anand raised his voice to interrupt him and suggest staying in his hometown for college, he was stopped by a steely resolve in Kunal's eyes which indicated that this matter was not up for debate.

Anand wanted to be supportive of his son's decision, but he did not agree with his stubborn wish to move away. Kunal insisted that he had to move away so that he could try to *find himself.* Anand could understand the youthful need to be different and to pursue a career of his choice. He told Kunal once again to reconsider his decision. He even admitted that he was being selfish and was greedy for more time with Kunal at home.

He even tried to bribe him.

"You can buy the sports car that you want."

Kunal only laughed at that.

"Or a motorcycle?"

"Dad, I know that you would buy me these things even if I don't stay here. Come on. You were young once. You can understand."

Anand was transferred for a moment to his days of struggle, the years of hard work that had usurped his youth. He tried to refrain from explaining to Kunal what it was really like, for him. The grueling nights of sheer hard work, the aching legs that struggled to walk home after waiting tables all day at a dinghy restaurant, the sheer poverty that had stained his youth stood as a dark memory imprinted into his mind. He could not even begin to tell Kunal about those years of his life.

"Ah, he thought to himself. How can the young people even understand about what it was like then?"

It was true that Anand wanted Kunal to stay in the house longer and complete his education in Bombay. However, he realized that this sentiment was purely out of fondness for his son.

He wanted Kunal to fly high and have everything his heart desired. He wanted him to explore the world and to travel and learn, experience life in its fullness. He wanted him to do all the things that Anand was deprived of due to lack of money.

He truly wanted all these things for Kunal, yet, he felt that he was not ready for him to leave.

It just seemed all too *soon*.

On the other hand, when Kanta heard about Kunal's decision, she went on a mission to do everything possible to try and keep her son as close to herself as possible. She started praying more than usual and Anand knew the reason for her prayers.

In her prayers, secret deals were being made with the Almighty so that Kunal would change his mind and decide to stay at home for his education. All the gods known to Divinity were being bribed with spiritual and material promises. Hefty donations were being offered to the local temple and the family priest.

Even Kunal was aware of this divine conspiracy against him. Laughing aloud, he told his mother to stop these endeavors. He promised her that he will come home to visit her every month. Still, Kanta kept on praying and hoping for him to change his mind. Lately, she had become more desperate and her discussions with Kunal resulted in a lot of tears which were followed by a dark brooding mood that persisted for days.

Finally, the day came to pack his suitcases. On a sad afternoon in April, with heavy hearts, Kanta and Anand drove him to the airport to fly to Delhi. Even Anand could not fight back his tears as they saw him disappear into the airplane.

The drive back home was sad and solemn. It seemed as if a dark silence had enveloped their lives. In a few minutes of his leaving, Kunal had taken away all the sunshine that had kept them alive so far.

To Anand, it seemed as if suddenly his life had become devoid of all purpose.

Kanta felt as if she was in a dark forest of gloom. She could not even cry any more. There was no remedy for her sorrow. She palpably felt the darkness enter her soul and make a permanent home in her heart.

CHAPTER
FORTY FIVE

IF WISHES WERE
HORSES . . . 1985

After Kunal had flown the coop to join Delhi College of Architecture, Anand realized the true meaning of an *empty nest*. He had heard people mention the phrase but never really thought much about it. Now, with Kunal gone, the house seemed darker. He found it depressing to be at home. The emptiness of Anand's life became more apparent and stared him in his face unabatedly.

He started to work even harder and stayed in the office for much longer as compared to before. There was really no need for him to work so much, but the option of going home was disappointingly unappetizing. He started working on acquiring and developing another office site. This would require rigorous work and consume his empty mind and fill up his evenings.

Of course, it required countless trips to the city office, in order to get multiple documents approved from the town planner. During each trip to her office, Anand secretly hoped to run into Sushma. On his trips to the city office, he felt as if he was walking in a dream. His step was lighter. On reaching Sushma's office, he was strangely self-conscious. His heart beat faster whenever he walked by her office. Even though, he tried hard not to peek at her desk, his mind always devised a way for him to see her; to find an excuse to go and talk to her about some documents vaguely connected to his new office site. His fascination for Sushma grew every day in spite of his repeated attempts to rein in his feelings. It was especially hard to forget Sushma when his conniving brain was constantly trying to invent ways to run into her.

To his credit, he had stopped his feet from heading towards her office on some days. On many occasions, he had driven to the city office and then driven off without even getting out of the car. He commended himself for doing the right thing on those days.

Even though his mind was constantly preoccupied with her thoughts, he knew that he would never ever be unfaithful to his wife. He was incapable of being characterless. His big disappointment with himself was that he *still* could not get her out of his mind.

He did not desire nor attempt to initiate anything resembling an affair. He had too many scruples. He had been brought up in a manner that such behavior would be considered unworthy of a member of the Sinha family.

Sushma, like all women, possessed the psychic intuition unique to her gender. It was easy for her to perceive his motive behind these coincidental meetings. She could also empathize with his mental struggle which seemed apparent in his obvious discomfort on meeting her. Oddly enough, his awkwardness was extremely flattering to her.

Anand, on the other hand, wondered about his actions and had analyzed his brain to bits.

Was he so depraved and immoral that he could not stay faithful to his wife?

Was his moral fiber so weak?

Was his religious belief in Lord Rama just a facade?

He could feel his mind struggling with his heart. At times he found himself talking aloud to no one in particular.

Yes. He was losing his mind!

According to Hindu religious teachings, a man is supposed to conduct his life as outlined by the life of Lord Rama. He should strive to be the ideal son, ideal husband and ideal man as depicted in the Ramayana. Anand found himself faltering and not being able to live up to that ideal. Rather, his behavior was immoral, and unbefitting of a married man.

Anand's work did not suffer. He was able to launch his new office successfully. His business stayed just as profitable as before. He was surprised at how he could stay so focused on his work when his head was in such great turmoil. Anand realized the capabilities of the human mind which could work so well at one level and constantly fail at another.

Also, his devoted care for Kanta did not change. He was always at her side until she improved.

Eventually, he stopped tormenting himself. Maybe, he thought, this fascination will wear itself out and eventually be forgotten.

He told himself that he was only human.

CHAPTER FORTY SIX

THE WIFE IS . . . THE FIRST TO KNOW 1985

It was Anand's general manager's son's birthday celebration in the evening and Anand was forced to attend it. After all, the son was born after many prayers *after three girls*. Each girl was supposed to be a boy, according to the predictions of the most revered family priest. Obviously, the birth of the girls was never celebrated as they had brought great disappointment to the family just by belonging to the female gender. A year ago, the birth of the *boy* had been God's answer to their intensified prayers and had wiped away all the unhappiness of the entire clan. All the possible love and attention was showered on this child who had brought light into the darkness and had made the family experience joy again!

Today, the boy was a year old and his manager pleaded, *"Sir, you have to come to our house and grace the occasion. I will not take no for an answer. We want you to give your blessings for our son."*

"Yes, Mr. Ratan. I will be there."

"And don't forget to bring the Mrs., Sir"

"Yes, yes! We will both be there, Mr. Ratan."

"This evening at 7 pm, don't forget, Sir! Thank you, Sir. Thank you very much. It will mean a lot if you are there tonight to bless him."

He had asked Kanta to be ready for this *momentous* occasion. She was happy and apprehensive at the same time. It was always a great deal of effort for her to get out of the house, especially in a social setting.

He reassured her, *"We will go for an hour at the most. He has been insisting a lot and will be really happy to see us there."*

Anand noticed Sushma the moment he entered Mr. Ratan's house. Apparently, she was remotely related to the family. Anand introduced her to Kanta and let them talk to each other as he went and joined the men in their usual discussions of politics and economy of the country. It never failed to surprise him how ordinary men during the day transformed themselves into learned political experts by the evening. Also, their wisdom became progressively more profound as the evening went on and the alcohol level in their blood increased.

His eyes kept going back to Sushma. She had brought a soft drink for Kanta and was now sitting next to her. They seemed to be having a pleasant conversation. He walked up to them to check on Kanta and she indicated that she was fine. Sushma politely enquired about his new office. He was surprised at how the awkwardness between then seemed to evaporate in the next few minutes of their conversation.

The birthday cake was brought out. The one candle was blown out by the aid of the overjoyed father while the unsuspecting child was looking at the crowd of well-wishers gathered around him. The cake was cut amid much fanfare and the child was blessed by everyone many times over.

Soon afterwards, they left the party. Kanta seemed happy. She really liked Sushma who had offered to take her to visit an exhibition for folk paintings in the city in the coming week. As he looked quizzically at his wife, she explained that she really wanted to go and that she was planning to let Sushma know about her disease. He shrugged and muttered faint words of encouragement to her.

He was a little puzzled at how peculiar the entire evening had been. He felt strangely uneasy.

Unknown to Anand, Kanta was extremely perceptive. She did not speak much but she knew Anand's darkest secrets. She knew her husband to be her kind caretaker, and she also knew him to be a calculating businessman. When she saw Anand looking at Sushma that night, Kanta knew that she had lost her husband to Sushma.

What Anand did not notice was the disappointment in Kanta's eyes as she watched him disappear into his study. The night had become a shade darker for her.

CHAPTER

FORTY SEVEN

A NEW NORMAL . . . 1986

Kanta and Sushma had become well acquainted at their brief meeting at the party.

When Sushma met Kanta, she could easily fathom how Kanta's medical condition had affected her life. She could sense that Kanta was lonely and led a limited life. Kanta's eyes carried a strange sadness that reminded Sushma of a mute animal suffering secretly in pain. Sushma truly wanted to help her. She was lonely herself. Ever since Suresh had passed away, *alcohol* had become Sushma's best friend. She thought that helping Kanta might help her feel good about herself, give her a purpose in life and assist her in quitting drinking again.

Why not try again? She had already quit four times that year so far!

She started befriending Kanta and talked to her on phone almost every other day. At Kanta's request, she started visiting her at her house. Kanta had become very reclusive because of her illness. She had started to withdraw from society and most of her time was spent in the house with her maid.

Now, Sushma took her shopping, even watch a movie or visit the theater; things that Kanta had loved doing in the past. Soon, it became commonplace for Sushma to visit Anand and Kanta's house once or twice a week.

Kanta had almost three seizures every month. Sushma accompanied Anand whenever Kanta had to be admitted to the hospital. Sushma stayed with her in the hospital most of the time until Kanta recovered from those episodes. Sushma, soon took over the role not only of Kanta's companion and friend, but also her medical caregiver. She occasionally accompanied Kanta to her doctor visits as well.

This was working out very well for Sushma, because she was able to quit drinking again...*for the fifth time that year alone!* Once again, she threw all her bottles and said goodbye to her flask.

A change had come over Kanta and she was starting to smile more. Almost instantly, Sushma had entered their household and made herself a permanent part of their lives.

Initially, Anand felt guilty about the whole situation. He wondered sheepishly, at times, at what Sushma had thought of his brief *courtship* of her. When he remembered his behavior, he felt angry at himself for acting in such an immature manner.

As weeks and months passed, he started to appreciate Sushma's help and effort. She had become Kanta's friend. Kanta appreciated Sushma's help and support in addition to the companionship that she provided. Anand was not awkward around her anymore. His schoolboy romance was moving backstage to the drama of their lives. He was extremely thankful for Sushma's friendship for Kanta.

"Yes, Sushma is a great ally for Kanta," Anand thought, trying to convince himself.

His infatuation had been a useless waste, he told himself. All the emotional turmoil and aggravation that he went through and for what purpose? He was never ever going to do anything to hurt his wife whom he cared for very deeply. He was very happy with his family and his social standing and would never do anything to tarnish his good name. He was able see Sushma once in a while, in a respectable setting. There was nothing secretive or improper about it and Kanta had a companion.

Maybe, this was the ideal situation: this *new normal.*

Once again, he immersed himself whole-heartedly into his work.

Everything changed in one night, however.

Kanta had been in the hospital for a week and had just returned home. She had contracted pneumonia and had a longer course of treatment to finish. Anand and Sushma had helped her back into her bed. The maid had brought soup for Kanta and Anand gave Kanta her medicine. She was on a new pill for epilepsy which made her extremely sleepy. As Kanta drifted off to sleep, Anand suggested that Sushma should stay for dinner before heading home.

It was almost midnight and Anand offered Sushma a ride back to her house, or to sleep in the guest room. They were both exhausted and Sushma decided to stay in the guest room upstairs. She waited till Anand and the maid left and reached for her flask in her purse. She had started drinking again. Unfortunately, the flask was near empty and she desperately sipped the last few drops. She had seen Anand's well stocked bar in the dining room and decided to get herself a drink. She slowly descended the stairs and crept stealthily towards the bar. She reached for the nearest bottle in the bar and was trying to open her flask in the dark when the light switched on. Anand stood at the door, looking at her.

He had heard rumors about her drinking and felt sorry for her. He poured a drink for both of them and invited Sushma to his room. He could see that Sushma needed more than just one drink to steady her shaking hands. After her third drink, which Sushma drank surprisingly fast, she changed into a different person. She was slurring her words and clung to Anand. Her arms were around his neck and she started kissing him sloppily. Anand was shocked and for a minute did not know how to react. He looked around, the house was dark and silent. He quietly shut the door and locked it from inside and led Sushma to the bed.

When he woke up in the morning, he was relieved to note that Sushma's car was not in the driveway.

He was disgusted with himself for giving in to temptation. Soon, however, he was able to rationalize that as well.

"If this is what she wants...."

CHAPTER
FORTY EIGHT

SUSHMA . . .

Sushma, at 45 years, was spry and appeared *really young* for her age, as her admirers told her. She was slightly built, had an ordinary yet pleasant face. There was a darkness behind her eyes that had set in ever since her husband, Suresh, died of cancer at the age of 48.

People who knew her, and there weren't many who did, could tell a visible change in her appearance from that day onwards.

They remembered a woman who was gregarious and fun. She was always talking too much, laughing too much, almost silly at times and getting giddy from her own talk and jokes. They remembered a woman who was well informed and was always getting into a discussion mostly to argue the opposing point of view. They remembered her getting passionate and emotional about her point of view almost to the point of tears. They remembered her using insulting language when talking about the politicians and the drug dealers. They remembered her proposal to train and arm every woman in the country with a gun so that they could deal with the sex offenders and the rapists themselves; without waiting for the slow as snails court system to dispense justice. They remembered her crying when Mother Teresa died. They remembered her being irreverent towards deeply held religious beliefs, challenging the power of religion and laughing at the superstitious bigwigs in the society. They remembered her sarcastically praising the business acumen of the so-called *gurus and the demigods* in the country who were becoming richer at the cost of their brainwashed impoverished followers.

She argued that truth was never absolute or what was taught to you. There were always multiple points of view and answers to the same question and they could all be true. She was shocked to learn and surmise that the world did not exist in black or white, right or wrong. There were a lot of grey areas in the world.

A lot of good people did bad things and yet, they were not only acceptable to the society, they were even revered and worshipped for their perceived holiness. It was amazing to see how bendable truth was, especially in the hands of politicians or religious leaders. Truth was so bendable a commodity that politicians were buying it to pay off their witnesses to abolish their crimes, religious leaders were preaching it to fill up their coffers with cash, rich people were covering it up with bribery in order to get even richer. In short, truth could be manipulated by different people to suit their needs.

The real truth existed almost in a hidden, unspoken form, unacknowledged, unseen and unwelcome mostly as it was not always beautiful, palatable or socially acceptable. Therefore, you could never believe people or what they said.

She could go on and on and on …to the point of exhausting the listeners.

And she was not even drinking at that time!

She was born and brought up in Lucknow, an old cultural city which was the center of Muslim culture in India. It was the city of *nawabs (lords)* and *tawaifs (prostitutes),* who were housed in kothas *(brothels where the trade was conducted with song and dance as a prelude).* Also, Lucknow was a city of sumptuous cuisine, beautiful, embroidered fabrics, a polite and well-spoken society and had nation's best educational centers and universities.

Her family was headed by her strict father, who worked very hard in a low paying government job, a mother who was a housewife. Her mother's great failure was that she had only been able to bear two daughters and **no son**. *(That would be her cross to bear for the rest of her life).* Money was always tight, and education was the only luxury, and that also in the most basic government school which was the cheapest in their area.

Her sister was three years younger, and they walked their way to school every day. There was no television in their house. The only entertainment was an old radio and the newspaper *(yes, people read the newspaper during those times!).* And there were books, all kinds of books in their house. These were left over from her father's school years, her uncles' books which never got thrown out of the house, most of them untouched by the students that they were intended for.

These books were kept stored in the glass lined cupboards which in a normal household would hold the beautiful china or a gold coated tea service. These books stayed on in the house decades after the said student had long graduated and moved on into their world!

There were books on engineering, as one of her uncles was an engineer; books on economics as another uncle was a PhD in Economics. There were books on philosophy, as her father's sister dabbled in philosophy, failed the exam and then ended up graduating in Home science, a relatively easier subject and considered infinitely more suitable to girls anyways. As a result, there were books on cooking. Another uncle graduated from the university with an advanced degree in physics (he was the most brilliant of the lot), therefore an abundant number of books relating to physics occupied one entire shelf.

Sushma read each and every book she could lay her hands on.

These books smelt as if they were buried in a deep hole where rats had been feasting on them. A few of them had certain parts of them visibly chewed up by the vermin. Yet, they were a vast treasure in Sushma's eyes. She read Emerson and Thoreau, Shakespeare and *GONE WITH THE WIND,* Steinbeck and Thomas Hardy, Sigmund Freud, Kahlil Gibran and also The Art of French Cooking, Mughlai Cuisine Made Simple and The Daily Psychologist. On certain days she read the concepts of rheology of blood flow and the science of bubbles, and there were days she read about the historical background of economic policies of OPEC countries with an occasional book about reinforced thrown in for good measure.

Much to her mother's discontent, she could spend a whole day reading. She had to wash her hands after reading these books, as they smelt awful. However, while reading, she felt transferred to a world which was almost dreamlike. Reading made her realize that there was a different world that existed outside of the confines of her everyday life. It existed unseen and unknown to her; as if somewhere in the middle of the earth and the sky. She was surprised to learn about the western world and how women were not as subservient to men as in India. She was also shocked to learn at that young age that women married many times *(three times in the case of Scarlett O Hara)*. The western religion also seemed strange as they worshipped only Jesus whereas in the Hindu religion you could worship a different god every day and there were temples dedicated to each special god.

The expanse of her mind widened beyond the reality of her everyday life through reading these books. She comprehended that her own existence in this world was miniscule and her little family that lived in a small house in a tiny little corner of the world was confined in a microsphere, of their own making. She knew that she would never spend her whole life living the same reality as her mother or her mother's mother before that. She knew that she would have to break free from this confined existence and venture further away and taste what life had to offer beyond their little house on Masjid Road.

No wonder, her sister said that her *head was in the clouds.*

"You are socially unacceptable," teased her sister who listened to her *"meaningless drivel",* pulled her hair, stuck out her tongue and ran outside to play with her friends, in that order.

Maybe, her sister was right. Maybe, she spent too much time reading. Unlike her friends, she had no idea what the current Bollywood movies were (her father would not let them watch movies anyways). Maybe, her clothes were too plain, there was lack of money and also lack of interest in fashion on her part. These facts however did not bother her as at the back of her mind she knew that she was destined for greater things.

Her mother was constantly puzzled by the things her older daughter *said* and constantly worried about the things that her younger daughter *did*. The older one was too plain to catch a good boy, she thought, but was hard working, quiet and respectful. The younger one was beautiful, cheerful and the darling of the family, yet she had no interest in her studies. At least, she will be able to find a good husband, she sighed with relief.

Soon, it was time to attend college. Sushma joined the university to start her Bachelor's in Literature. It was her first day in the university and she realized how out of place she looked and felt. The real world outside of her books was unpredictable, harsh and severe. She felt herself to be too plain and the target of many pointed looks from the popular girls. Yet, she was happy to be at the university and found the campus to be beautiful and college life to be full of surprises.

There were the rich girls who were fashionable and always had interesting places to go to and exciting parties on weekends to recount their experiences from. There were the girls who were from extremely traditional families who frowned at the rich girls and secretly bitched about them. She would sit with the group of *have-nots* and criticize them as well. She felt like a hypocrite, though. Sushma secretly envied the rich girls' lives. She knew that she would be immensely happy to have their lifestyle. *"What is so wrong with stepping out of a shiny car anyways?"*

College was what made her realize that there was a world that existed beyond the musty pages of her books. A world that was full of music, makeup, movies and of course, *boys*. She was fascinated by everything. For the very first time she was introduced to the popular music and not just Indian Bollywood music, but English music. She had bought a small stereo and her friends were kind enough to lend her their music and she was completely enthralled by it. Also, now she was introduced to the concept of eating out. At home her family was always thrifty and eating out was never an option. Now, even with her meager allowance she could afford to go out with her friends and eat out once in a while, though not at a very fancy restaurant.

Additionally, being at college introduced her to the opposite sex. This was another novelty for her as her extremely sheltered existence at home had been devoid of much exposure to boys. She was immediately aware of the attractive ones in her class and those could be counted on her fingers. The only tragedy was that the good-looking ones were never very intelligent and vice versa. There were just a handful of them who were good looking and intelligent, and of course they were looking for the trendy, rich and beautiful girls and she unfortunately did not fall in that category, by any standards.

The ones that liked her were too average for her and she was too average for the ones she wanted to be liked by.

Another factor that held her back was her middle-class upbringing. She had grown up with the idea of girls being virtuous and pure. Morality was almost synonymous to avoiding unnecessary interaction with boys. These ideas were drilled into her mind and her subconscious.

No one in the history of their family had ever had a *boyfriend.* It was a word that was not even mentioned in their house for the fear that if it was spoken out loud, the girls would become immoral and lose their virtue! Everyone in their family, all the cousins, boys or girls, had arranged marriages. After marriage, all of them had two children each and had well-manicured families. Her mother constantly reminded her that they were all *sukhi (*happy*)* and were well settled. This was the goal in the family, to have the girls be *well settled,* and the only way to do that was to have them married off to a suitable boy! This was ingrained into her mind and her psyche since her childhood.

Therefore, she explained to her friends, she would never have a boyfriend. She did not have the DNA for it because of her upbringing. This made her coin her first witticism, *"You can take a girl out of middle class, but you can never take the middle class out of a girl."*

It was cheesy, yet she quoted it many times around her friends and thought that it made her sound humorous. They laughed at her comments briefly, while preening themselves and craning their necks over her head to look pretty just in case a *boy* happened to be around.

Luckily for her, college was academically easy for her. Her Baccalaureate in Literature was easy, she had a natural affinity for literature and her teachers recognized her ability to turn a simple assignment into a distinct piece of writing. Her teacher was extremely impressed by her writing and often circulated her assignment among the class for the rest of the students to read as an example of a *perfect* piece of writing. She was just having too much fun in college and eagerly awaited the next assignment to immerse herself in.

One day, her teacher was so impressed by her essay on Emerson that she asked her to accompany her to the Principal's office to discuss her future. The Principal was a sari clad strict woman who inspired fear and was not well liked among the students. Sushma followed her teacher reluctantly into the Principal's office. This was definitely not the way she wanted to spend her lunch hour.

As she entered her office, she was introduced to the Principal by her teacher. She signaled her to sit across her huge desk. She did not waste much time in pleasantries and got straight to the point.

"We are really impressed with your language skills and your knowledge of literature. What are your future plans?"

"I am sorry. I am not sure at this point," babbled Sushma.

"Well, we were thinking that you should finish your Masters' Degree in Literature and then you could take up a job as a Lecturer in English at our institution. You know with time you would become a Professor. You should talk to your parents and let me know if you would like to pursue that. In about three years we will have a vacancy as Mr. Chadha is going to retire. I think this would be a great opportunity for you."

"Oh, thank you for the offer," Sushma said uncertainly. She had seriously not thought about her employment so far.

"Can I talk to you about this in the next week? This will give me some time to discuss it with my parents."

"Sure, in the meantime I have a few students who have requested tutoring in English from you, to help them with their homework. Of course, they will pay you. Let me know about that as well."

This was extremely exciting for her. She discussed it with her parents who were overjoyed to hear the news. Yes, now they could see that one of their daughters would definitely get *well settled*. Having a job as a lecturer in the university is not only desirable, it was also very respectable. These jobs were not easy to get, definitely not without *sifarish* (recommendation from a powerful politician, usually obtained after a hefty bribe).

That was how Sushma started to make money, by tutoring her junior students. She was busy now, with her own studies and teaching the students. These girls did not really want to be taught, they mainly wanted her to do their assignments for them. Some of them were really not well versed in the English language and the others did not want to be bothered about learning. They just wanted to finish college so that they could look respectable on their matrimonial *advertisement*.

The money was not much but it was enough, for her to buy books, music, a few trendy outfits, to eat out once in a while. She was suddenly acceptable among the popular girls and she loved it. There were invitations to parties, birthdays, picnics, movies and cricket matches. She chose the ones where she would have to spend the least money. Her father did not approve of her clothes and her new friends. He repeatedly shook his head but could not say much because she was actually contributing money to the family. Also, he trusted her. He knew that in her heart she would always be his older child who would always do the right thing. He knew that she was cognizant of the family expectations and would actually make him proud one day. He was aware of her superior intelligence and was secretly proud of her. He believed that even though the constant reading in her younger years had refined her thinking, her heart was in the right place. By working for money, she was already challenging the norms of their household, but *what is youth without rebellion?*

Sushma was loving her life at that point. She was in the swing of things and she was having a good time. She was moving with the popular crowd now and initially had a few moments of self-consciousness as she compared her life to her new friends' wealthy lifestyle. However, she got over them pretty quickly. She never pretended to be one of them and openly told them that she did not own a car, she had an old *moped*. She could not have parties in her house, and she wasn't able to go to the local *gymkhana* or the prestigious *golf club*. Her friends however accepted her because what she did not have in money, she made up with her sparkling wit and conversation. She was lighthearted, well-spoken and a good friend to have around and that seemed to be enough. Also, she was probably a refreshing change for them as well. She did not have airs, was never showing off her new jewelry or clothes, mainly because she did not have *any!*

Between her tutoring, classes and busy social life, time flew as if it was on wings. Her Baccalaureate in Literature was finished soon after and she sent in applications to pursue Master's in Classic Literature at the prestigious Lucknow

University. When her acceptance letter arrived, she was not really surprised.

It was in her second year there that she met Suresh. He was doing his Masters' in Economics and was the same age as her. They even had the same birthday! He was struck by her, she could tell. He was found lingering outside the Literature building which was actually in a different wing as compared to the Economics section. He somehow suddenly appeared at the exact time of her leaving the building to walk up to the bus station. For days, he rode on his noisy motorcycle alongside her as she walked. Both of them decided that it looked really odd and silly and that she should just accept a ride from him; it was a two-minute ride anyways. By the next month, he started showing up at her bus station in the morning as well to drop her off at her building and then drive on to his.

"Oh, this is exactly on my way," was his explanation.

He was nice, pleasant to look at and absolutely not interested in literature. She told him that literature had been her lifelong passion! He was planning to never ever teach in his life and she wanted to be a Professor! He wanted to finish his Masters' and start his own business in IT with his best friend who was finishing his degree in computer engineering, and he could not wait to do that.

"Oh boy!" she thought to herself. "We are not compatible at all!"

Yet, he kept showing up day after day, asking about how her day, what her plan was for the next day and so forth, insisting on driving her. Soon, he became a part of her life and so much of a routine that she did not even think about it twice. It was her sister who pointed out that they were on their way to becoming a couple; actually, they already were!

"Hmmm. Let me clarify it for you. Do you see anyone else?

No.

Does he offer motorcycle rides to any other girl?

No.

The evidence, members of the jury, is overpowering and beyond a reasonable doubt.

I rest my case," she finished with an exaggerated flourish in her virtual courtroom. (She was planning to go the law school and every conversation with her was an argument that needed to be won in an imaginary court of law).

Of course, initially she laughed it off. Later, however, the wisdom of her sister proved correct and she was not half surprised when he proposed to her. It was really very odd to be asked to consider him seriously as a life partner. She wished she could laugh the whole evening off and make the question disappear. However, she let him know that she could not take such a decision without discussing with her family. She was strangely flattered and amused.

She was in deep thought while walking home that day. She felt that her world had altered in an unparalleled manner. However, the more she thought about it the more anxious she became. She realized that she was treading in unfamiliar territory. She had so far interacted with him in a casual, fun sort of a relationship. Now, everything seemed so serious and suddenly had acquired huge importance. Earlier, they could be friends, or just two people who had crossed each other's path for a short duration in their life. Now, this had to become a more permanent and immutable part of her life.

Their friendship, which earlier had endless possibilities had now shrunk and become limited in dimension as now it would be heading towards *marriage*, a word that inspired fear in her.

Her universe seemed to be closing in on her. It was as if a huge block of concrete was sitting on her chest. She felt suffocated by her own thoughts and was unable to breathe by the time she reached home. As she entered the doorstep, she realized that she was having a panic attack.

That day, she did not tell anyone. She knew that she could not handle discussing it just yet. She feigned illness and did not go to the university the next day. She dragged her sister into the room and told her. After telling her to wipe the silly grin off her face, she asked her what she should do.

"You are asking me?" She gasped. *"I don't know. Well, for starters, is he okay looking?"*

"He is ok to look at."

Her sister saw the panic in her eyes and realized that this was serious.

"Didi, do you like him?"

"I am just not sure. I feel very anxious and just don't know."

"Well, then just wait and see how you feel in a week. Stall him! If you don't have the answer in a week then he is not for you."

"What would you do, if you were in the same situation?"

Her sister hesitated.

This was delicate. She did not want to blurt out what came to her mind, which was, "*I would not marry the first person who came along and asked me!*"

Rather, she said, formulating her words very carefully, "*I would do just that. I would ask for more time and consider.*"

She knew Sushma too well. She was too much into the books and she could not see her finding herself a boyfriend, not with her moral, intellectual and weird scruples and expectations. If she did not choose this Suresh person, the next option would be an arranged marriage. Anything was better than arranged marriage. She shuddered inwardly at the thought of the word - *arranged marriage* and patted Sushma's hand consolingly.

She called Suresh the next day and did just that. She asked for a week and requested to be left alone for a week so she could consider it very seriously. He tried to lighten the mood by saying that he did not want to frighten her, that they could still be friends, that it was not that big a deal. She assured him that it may not be a serious matter to him, but it was to her. She wanted to take some time and decide, and that he should understand that.

She walked around in this strange bubble that was wrapped around her. All the trees and flowers on her way seemed to be devoid of color. Even though it was the middle of spring, everything seemed a little pale and faded and she walked around in a daze. Finally, it dawned on her: it wasn't that she did not like Suresh, it was just the idea of being married to him that was frightening her.

In all fairness, the idea of being married to anyone was frightening, and there was no way she could go through her life without getting married. Not with the reminders from her parents, *"Beta, we should soon be looking for a boy for you,"* but also the prying faces of her relatives, always with the question, *"So, any good boys for Sushma so far?"*

Well, if she was going to get married to anyone, it might as well be Suresh. At least she knew him, and it would be better than going through the trauma of arranged marriage, which she knew would break her. The mere thought of being put on display and being interviewed by the various relatives of the *boy* was nauseating in itself and it made her shudder involuntarily.

Marriage, in that middleclass world of hers was a bitter pill to be swallowed, a deed to be done to liberate yourself, and also to liberate your parents of the burden that was placed on their shoulders the day you were born in the form of a daughter and not a *son*.

She should not complain much, though. There were multiple horror stories of what happened to some girls in her neighborhood. A girl, just a year junior to her, that she had tutored, was literally burnt alive by her own mother when she found out that she had a boyfriend. Another cousin who was brilliant, was denied permission to go out of town to join a medical school by her father, who feared that she might get *overly ambitious* (sic) if she left town to seek higher education.

These were confusing times, she thought. Girls were being encouraged to be educated but not too educated. They were being told to venture out onto the world and yet stay indoors. They were being told that they were equal to men and yet they were told not to assert themselves too much. There were laws being enacted every day to provide security to women, to make them safer and yet every girl's parents expected her to be home by sundown. The very police that were supposed to provide protection to women was involved in criminal conduct against them. No wonder, it was safer for a woman to be married and then the parents felt that they had done their duty towards their daughter and could now heave a sigh of relief. Sushma's parents had not just her to marry off, they also had to take care of her younger sister. She could almost feel the yoke of their burden choking her and crushing her shoulders.

Yes, she would get married, just to make her parents' life easier, if for nothing else. Yes, things could be way worse. At least she was going to have a job, a career, her own money and some independence. Maybe, it would not be so bad after all.

Maybe, then she could live her life and work towards what she really wanted to do and focus on her life and career.

She called Suresh and told him that she was ready to discuss marriage. He met her at the coffee shop, and it was terribly awkward for both of them. They were going to talk about being together for the rest of their lives! The only image that kept her grounded was the scary prospect of *arranged marriage*.

She put a cheery smile on her face and saw that Suresh cheered up as well. It was going to be just fine. At least, he cared for her. He would be just right for her, she knew at that moment. He was way better than whatever her parents or relatives might conjure up as a suitable boy from a suitable caste for her.

"My answer is yes."

He was very happy to hear her decision. He was already planning their life, their future, where he wanted to live eventually, what kind of a job package he was hoping for from his first job at a major bank, how his uncle knew a minister who would talk to the general manager at a reputed bank to get him the entry level position and how he was going to work really hard from then on and make a big name for himself and then he was going to save up money and then go into business with his best friend as the real money in the long term was going to end in the computer business.

Halfway, through his animated discussion, she found herself thinking that this was going to be even better than expected. He was so wrapped up in his own plans that he was probably going to leave her alone and she could do what she wanted; teach literature. She kept nodding at his many plans, he seemed as if he had his whole life mapped out and she was just one small piece of his big jigsaw puzzle. He really did not even need her; he could have filled that position with any girl. However, in her life, he would be a vast improvement from who her parents might choose for her.

So, this is how that came about. The prelude to their engagement was a very well thought out decision, devoid of much emotion and full of extreme practical wisdom. Her parents were very happy to hear the news. Not only was this extremely timely, but Suresh's family was also well known in the community and was relatively well off. The date for the family meeting was set within the month.

Suddenly, things became very happy and busy at the same time in both the households. A priest had been consulted and the marriage had to be accomplished under a very short auspicious timeline. This had been mapped out based upon the Hindu mythological charts which provided guidance to the periods when the divine celestial powers were going to be the most generous with their blessings towards this wondrous union.

Clothes needed to be bought and jewelry too. All sorts of relatives and neighbors were being consulted. There were multiple days of fittings and trying out clothes. The budget for the wedding was mapped out and was breached many times. All of Sushma's savings were tapped into. Her mother's secret stash of cash was retrieved from the bottom of a steel box which was kept hidden under a pile of winter clothes. Her father happily informed them of the savings plan that he had started for this very day in the bank for Sushma since she was five years old. Luckily the money had grown nicely over these years and they will be able to have a reasonably nice if not an extravagant wedding.

Within a month the auspicious lining up of planets and the rising of a certain special star was predicted by the priest and the wedding day was fixed. Wedding cards were printed and distributed, the menu was selected for the big day, the neighborhood women were invited to sing wedding songs, dancing was encouraged in their house, which seemed extremely strange as her father had never allowed loud music to be played in their house. All the ceremonies and the traditional wedding rites were outlined and everyday everybody went to bed exhausted.

Finally, the supremely auspicious day arrived and with much ceremony and emotion the wedding was conducted. When it was over, everyone heaved a sigh of relief.

CHAPTER
FORTY NINE

SUSHMA

The days immediately following the wedding, were a series of fast-moving events that left her in a pleasant tizzy. Years later when she reminisced about that time, it was extremely hard for her to remember the details, even if she forced her mind to do so. She remembered hurriedly packing her stuff to leave her home, teary eyed and in complete silence. Her sister and her mother looked at her through their own tears, as her father was paying the cab driver.

Suresh and Sushma were going to move to a rental apartment which was small and cramped and close to Suresh's new job. Suresh was excited; the idea of an exciting future that lay ahead of them energized him immensely. However, his parents were saddened by their son's decision to leave them so soon after his wedding.

He would meet them every weekend, Suresh had reassured them. Sushma was secretly happy that she did not have to live in a joint family.

Of course, Suresh had planned well and thought of everything. He had found that their commute would be half an hour each; to his office in Ganj and in the opposite direction for her to the University. He had sat down and discussed their finances on their first night, totaling up their income and how much they could save every month after paying for their expenses. He wanted to save enough so that in two years they could make a move to Bombay, and then he would start his joint venture with his school time friend, Ashish. He had already saved some money and as really passionate about his plans.

Her husband really was really focused on launching their financial life. Needless to say, they could not even think of having a child just yet. *That would be a goal to be set for their third year!*

Sushma really did not imagine herself to be capable of a successful childbearing experience. She had heard horror stories about labor pains and harbored a latent fear that she would die during childbirth. She was always in awe of the women who survived the surreal ordeal of childbirth.

There was nothing wrong with being practical, but to calculate your future child out of the equation for three years seemed a little cold hearted to Sushma.

All in all, Sushma was truly proud of her brand-new husband; he had laid down the blueprint of their future with absolute certainty.

Soon they fell into their routine. She was happy; Suresh was very caring and thoughtful and very loving towards her. They would come back from work and share their stories. She would cook a simple meal and he helped clean up. This was followed by watching news on television, sometimes a movie and then they went to bed. Sex was gratifying, they were always obsessive about contraception, and life was easy. There were no conflicts in this simple scheme of things.

Two years passed quickly. The money that was saved as per Suresh's calculations was saved and they moved to Bombay, which was further away from her hometown of Lucknow.

The move from her childhood city Lucknow to the gargantuan Bombay almost broke her spirit.

Bombay (now renamed as Mumbai, its original Marathi name) is a huge city, large enough to reduce any human being to an ant on the wall. In the huge sea of people that spilled onto its streets, it is easy to lose yourself, your identity and your way. She took a long time to adjust to this city and however hard she tried, she could not land a teaching job at any college or university. You really had to know someone important to land any job or be able to shell out a lot of money as a bribe.

Living in Mumbai was going to be an arduous challenge for her. She missed her job in Lucknow. She had made a name for herself in the university and was on her way to becoming a junior faculty member. She also was tutoring students for additional money and was very happy. Their apartment in Lucknow was not big but was spacious and clean. Here, living conditions were very bad. The one room apartment they had was just that. It was one room, and the different corners of this space were a kitchen which was really a hot plate, a living area which was a small sofa and one tiny table, a bedroom which was just a small cot with a bed sheet and two pillows, and a dressing area which was a mirror on the wall. Thank God they had running water; there were areas in their neighborhood where there was no running water.

She tried really hard to make the best of her living situation, but every time she looked around, she realized that they were *poor, and getting poorer by the day.* Most of their savings were now used up in the small business venture that Suresh and Ashish had launched. Their business involved selling cooking stoves that used natural gas, which was a relatively new industry. The demand was really low and at this point they were contacting private buyers for their sales. An entire month passed by without a single sale. All their savings were rapidly dwindling and there was no possibility of a job for either Suresh or her.

Three months had passed by and they were down to their last few pennies. Her desperation reached a new high point when she saw that their savings account had to be closed. Suresh contacted his father for more money. Sushma started combing the newspapers for vacancies. She swallowed her pride and applied for a meager secretarial position in the town planner's office.

Luckily, she was hired, and she started working the very next week. The job was not lucrative in any way, but they were at least able to meet their expenses. *Barely!* Her heart longed to go back to her teaching job, but that was not a possibility.

Suresh and Ashish had accepted defeat and shut down their business as it just did not take off. Suresh was frustrated and his failure had marked his temperament. They were now starting to have fights, he was unemployed and depressed, and they had to survive with the money brought in by her income. She also started looking for tutoring opportunities, and with great difficulty found two students who wanted to be home tutored. The commute was about an hour each way but the money was needed. She suggested to Suresh that he should look for a job and this was always met with an argument and followed by a long fight and a loud shouting match usually ensued after.

They were not happy anymore. They looked tired and defeated. Her cheeks were getting more sunken in with each passing day. His face was getting furrowed with anxiety and dejection.

Two years after their move to Mumbai, she told Suresh that she wanted to go and visit her parents. He did not stop her. He did not want to accompany her, either. She knew that he was embarrassed and did not want to acknowledge his failure to his parents. He, however, did not stop her from going.

She spent two weeks at her parents' home, was just happy to be away from the squalor that her life had become and lied about how happy they were. Her mother believed her lies happily, was a little worried about how thin she looked and cooked her favorite foods. Her father had a million questions to ask about Suresh and she answered them again and again with gloriously fabricated lies: about how well his business had taken off and how bright his prospects were and how he was so busy that he just could not get away to visit them, even for a few days.

Her sister was finishing up her degree in law and had already chosen who she was going to marry, a fellow lawyer, not from their caste, but she did not care. She also did not believe any of the lies that Sushma told her.

"I am not really a fool. It is easy to see you are not happy. What is wrong?"

Sushma's eyes teared up and she told her about what was actually going on - about the failed business, their lack of money and their meager source of income. Also, how difficult Suresh was to live with, since he was bitter about his lack of employment.

"Well, things will be ok. Just keep working at it, love each other and somehow everything will be fine."

For the first time, Sushma felt as if her sister was the older of the two. Somehow these words were the most encouraging advice and she literally took these words to her heart. She was strangely empowered by the simple optimism of that sentence. At the end of the two weeks, she felt as if she had become stronger, and she was not as dejected as before when she boarded the train for her long journey back to Mumbai to return to her husband.

She felt sorry for him but she vowed that she was never going to leave him alone. Sooner or later, he will wake up and realize that a job, any job, would be better than to just sit at home and do nothing.

She worked hard and listened patiently as he discussed his next venture: opening a computer academy to teach basic typing and computer skills to students after high school.

Ashish had found two other partners and they were willing to provide them the money at 10% interest. The expense was considerable but this time they already had twenty enrollees. Suresh and Ashish would be the instructors. Suresh had been taking classes and training from Ashish and they had also visited other academies. There was a demand building up in the new workforce as basic computer skills were starting to be considered as a necessity in the emerging job markets.

He was getting excited about this as he spoke. She realized that he was actually asking for her permission to start this. There was no starting expense, but they would have to make monthly payments to their partners. The loan had to be paid off in the next three years otherwise there would be a large penalty. According to their calculations, if they could have forty enrollees on a constant basis, they would be able to own the business in three years.

It was a worrisome proposal, she could see that it was almost a gamble, yet it was better than doing nothing. She told Suresh that she was going to support his decision as long as he promised to take up a job if this did not work out and he promised her that.

The academy was really a small room on the top of a beauty parlor in their neighborhood. It was dirty, but there were twenty-five chairs, five old typewriters and two computers. A large blackboard was placed facing the classroom and that was pretty much it.

They started in the hot and humid month of June. The very first month they had to buy five more chairs and an additional computer. Each session was three months at a time and classes lasted eight hours a day. Suresh, who had a major in Economics was teaching a computer course and she, a lecturer in English, was working in the town planner's office as a secretary. So much for her useless Masters' degree in Classic English Literature!

Suresh worked hard, at times too hard. He mastered the subject matter and was devoting more than three hours to each class. He was deeply involved in making the students learn and encouraged them not to leave the class unless they understood everything. Ashish also worked hard and managed the accounts well.

As their students were happy, more enrollees started to join the academy. The first session was a huge success, and enrollment for the next session was encouraging. Finally, money started coming in and Suresh being the same old frugal person that he was, started paying off the loan. He still did not own a vehicle other than a bicycle. She was still taking the bus to her work.

More and more students were calling for enrollment and they had to hire a secretary to answer phone calls. By the time the third year rolled in they were expanding and had to rent a larger space, to be able to seat fifty people. They also hired another instructor.

Finally, with their carefully saved money, after five years of marriage, they started looking for a better flat to live in. It was exciting to move into a two-bedroom flat which had an elevator in the building and a guarded entrance. This was in a brand-new building and had a swimming pool and a gym in the clubhouse. They also bought their first car, it was a used car, but now they did not have to walk everywhere in the heat of humid Mumbai.

She did not have to work anymore, Suresh told her fondly. She however wanted to continue to work. Her job was easy, she had been promoted to an assistant manager, which meant more money for her. She enjoyed her routine and was happy to continue with her work. Literature and her love for it seemed to belong to an era from long, long ago. She had not read a book in years and her connection to the literary world was now a thing of the past.

She had gone back to see her parents every year. Her sister was now married and lived with her husband in the southern part of the city. She was happy, she said. He doted on her, as long as she lived in the joint family with his parents. He was the only child, and his parents were easy going, or at least so she said. All these statements seemed to be too good to be true. Her own life had never been that easy or that perfect and she found her stories hard to believe. She did not question her too much. She told her repeatedly that if she needed her, she was always there to help.

It was now eight years since she had been married to Suresh. Finally, money was not an overwhelming problem anymore. Now, her worry was trying to have a baby. Her younger sister was already pregnant, and everyone was hoping for a boy, and she had let everyone know that yes, the ultrasound confirmed it, that it was actually (*glory be to the greatest God*) --a BOY!

This was great news, but it was also added pressure on Sushma to have a baby. It was almost embarrassing to let everyone know that they were trying to have a baby and had been trying for the last three years. She never thought that having a baby would have been such a hard task to accomplish, especially in India. The bulging population of the country is a testament to the fact that it is an over fertile country. The population explosion had the government publicly begging people to have fewer children. On the other hand, Sushma and Suresh were somehow managing to fail in that department.

She suspected that Suresh's smoking had something to do with it. He had become a heavy smoker lately and smoke was everywhere in their house. Initially, it bothered her but now she had become used to it. He had become thinner lately, was always working and lately had a chronic cough. She believed that his general poor health had something to do with their inability to conceive. She had told him many times that he should quit, and he said he would try but actually he never wanted to quit. It was the only thing that seemed to bring him calm and relaxation. Lately, life had become easier, but it seemed as if the initial years of struggle had scarred his spirit and left him with many unsealed wounds. He was not the one to talk too much but he had become more withdrawn and silent lately.

She also had begged him to see a doctor, but he smiled and gestured her away every time she said that. *"He was fine,"* he told her dismissingly and there was no need for her to worry about him. She was not able to argue with him beyond a certain point. If she argued too much, he tended to fall silent and shut himself up in the confines of his personal space and it was impossible for her to permeate through that barrier of silence.

Another span of two years passed. Her sister was now a mother of one bouncing baby boy and pregnant yet again.

This time around the prayers for a boy were not so fervent as she already had a boy and had done her duty towards the continuation of her husband's dynasty! Now, she could have a daughter and still be worshipped and loved in the eyes of everyone. No one even bothered to ask Sushma about her progress in the childbirth arena.

Sushma was getting increasingly concerned worried about Suresh. He had lost more weight and was becoming visibly weaker. He was coughing even more. The day he coughed up blood was when she forcibly took him to the nearby hospital. The doctor took a lengthy history, looked accusingly at Sushma, asking her why he was not brought to the doctor any sooner. His chest X-ray was suspicious for cancer, he told her.

It took a really long time to register in her mind. When she realized the horrendous implications of this statement, she broke down. She called Suresh's parents and they were by his bedside within the next two days. The cancer had spread to his bones and to his brain. The cancer specialist met with them and offered advanced treatment options which could add more weeks to his life but could not cure the cancer. It was just too far gone.

Suresh did not have the luxury to be shielded from the truth. He was witness to the initial diagnosis and the result of every disappointing test that he was subjected to afterwards. He heard the discussion of the end of his own life with unbelieving ears. He watched the drama of his life fade away and was now forced to visualize the soon to ensue, gory dance of death.

He was surprised at how soon his life had been sucked out of him. Moreover, he felt sad for Sushma. When he looked at her worried eyes constantly filled with tears, he felt guilty for leaving her too soon down the road of life. He felt as if he had failed to provide her with any happiness or comfort and was now becoming a sad burden for her. He thought that he had brought her no real joy; a huge financial struggle which had now eased after a huge struggle. He felt that he had deprived her of a child and was leaving her alone and devoid of all joy.

She walked around all day, talking to the nurses and the doctors, running to get the medicines that were needed from the nearby chemist's shop. Her eyes had become haggard and there were dark shadows underneath them. Her clavicles jutted out from underneath her neck. There were hollows in her cheeks and worry etched into her forehead. It seemed as if she had a cancer growing within her soul. Watching her like this saddened him immensely. When he saw her haggard body walk down the hallway of the hospital towards him, looking more tired and thinner from the previous day, his heart broke many times over.

Silently, he started praying fervently for his own death. Even when she was consulting with every possible oncologist in the hospital in the unrealistic hope of prolonging his life, he talked silently for his hastened death. He had become very weak now and since his admission to the hospital he could not even get out of bed by himself. He needed help to be washed up, changed into his clothes, to turn in his bed and now he could not even feed himself. He was declining rapidly and had unbearable pain due to spreading of cancer to his bones.

How he would have welcomed a night of uninterrupted pain-free sleep! He tried not to pity himself and tried to save that for his exhausted wife and his disheartened parents. He saw the disappointment that his disease had brought upon everyone.

Finally, after a full thirty days of being in the hospital, he signaled to Sushma that he wanted to speak to her without his parents around him. She sat on his bed and he attempted to hold her hand in his skeletal hand. It surprised him again, the very lifelessness of him. He told her that it was time to let him go and to set his spirit free. It was frustrating to see that Sushma did not understand him for his first few attempts at this conversation. He had to spell it out for her in his weak hoarse voice.

"I want to die, Sushma. I am not able to deal with this pain and discomfort any further. Please set me free," he beseeched her.

She could not believe her own ears.

He was asking her for permission to die, she kept thinking. It was hard to imagine the end of their life together even before it had truly begun. He had just managed to become financially successful. They had just paid off all their loans and were even thinking of adopting a child. They had just planted their small little window garden (just a few tomatoes as none of them really had a green thumb). They had not even decided on the color of paint in their new office building that he had acquired for expansion of his coaching center.

They had just started to socialize and now they had started making friends. They had just become part of the kitty party culture and had acquired membership to the prestigious gymkhana club. They had just started their bridge and poker nights on Wednesdays. She had started enjoying their new life where there was no worry of money. She had started a social work group to help women who suffered from infertility. She had started visiting an orphanage twice a month to take food and clothes for the children and also to secretly hope to adopt one of them.

Her mind wandered to a million places before she heard him again.

He was shaking her arm with his trembling hand and she woke up from her reverie and looked at him again.

"Can you bring me the file which is locked in your steel cabinet?"

She was still in a daze.

"Right now," he almost whispered before lapsing into a bout of coughing.

She sped home and got the file. He made her sit next to her and gave her the details of their finances, the banks, the accounts in businesses, the number of their accountant and his will.

"He has a will?" she couldn't believe that. *"How could a forty-eight-year-old man have a will? When did he prepare for all this? How long had he known all this was going to happen?"*

She felt terribly guilty. She was overcome by the feeling that this was all her fault. If she had not complained so much about their lack of money, maybe he would have smoked less, drank less, worked less and taken care of his health more. She was healthy and strong. He was wasted and dying, and it was all her fault.

She felt his wiry hand touch her arm again.

"Please call Ashish if you have any questions. You know he will help you."

He took her hand and looked at her lovingly.

"You have taken care of me so well. I could never have asked for a better wife. Always remember that even when we fought, I loved you so much."

He continued to gaze into her eyes silently for a long time. She stroked his hair away from his weary eyes and held his hand. She watched him until his face grimaced and contorted in severe pain.

"Can you have the nurse come in. My pain is back, and I want to rest, forever. Please help me get out of this pain. I don't want to live with this pain anymore. Please understand. I want to die. Let me go."

She ran outside and called the nurse to administer the pain medicine. She phoned his doctor and let him know that he could not tolerate the pain anymore. The doctor happened to be in the hospital and came over to speak with her. They decided that it may be the best for him to be transferred home with a nurse to provide 24-hour pain control. He would at least be comfortable.

The doctor looked her in the eye and told her calmly, *"I don't expect him to make it beyond a week. I want you to be prepared for the worst."*

She called his parents and the next day they brought him home. He had to be medicated heavily with morphine and was barely conscious in the next few days. She was with him, constantly by his bedside. It was comforting to see him free of pain. He opened his eyes to see her only twice in the next five days. When he opened his eyes, they were vacant, and his listless gaze did not acknowledge her presence.

On the sixth day he was gone.

Forever.

She was left with sorrow, complete emptiness and immense guilt that was unbearable. She was dogged with the constant nagging question in her mind.

"Did she cause his death?

Could she have done something different?

What if she had taken him to the doctor sooner?

What if she had fought with him more about the cigarettes?

What if she had taken his cough more seriously? What if ....?"

She decided to stay on in the same house. She kept working at her job. It gave her a reason to wake up in the morning to get out of the house. She sold the rest of the business to Ashish and he helped her invest half of it and keep the rest in a savings account. Her maid and servant stayed with her.

This was also the time when she started drinking.

Heavily.

In the beginning, it was easy. She just had to wait till her maid was asleep and she would go into the living room, put the tv on and pour herself a glass of wine. When all the wine was gone, she started with the whiskey, and the rum and the gin and the beer. In about a period of six months their well-stocked bar was empty.

She rejoined her Ladies' Bridge club. Wednesday evenings were now spent at one of the member's houses drinking and playing cards. Also, it was easy to have one of them buy alcohol for her. She managed to keep her bar well stocked and her drinking a fairly well-kept secret from her family and her coworkers. Of course, *all* her friends knew.

Her sister could not understand why she kept on working at her low paying job. Her income from the interest in her savings account alone was more than what she earned at her job. She tried to explain to her sister that it was important for her to have some routine in her life. Her job made her get out of the house, and she welcomed the time away from the house, because the moment she stepped back into the house she slipped into the now familiar pattern of drinking and watching tv. She did not care anymore. Her maid and her servant both knew that *memsahib* had started drinking daily.

Her parents had tried to have her come back and stay in Lucknow with them, but she could not go back to that life anymore. They *need* not ever know about her drinking. That would be moral death for them, especially her father. She did not want them to see her like this. Alcohol did wonders to dull the pain. More importantly, it filled the empty hours in her days, and the months and years that followed.

CHAPTER FIFTY

I NEED A FRIEND . . . 1980

Meeting Anand was a pleasant surprise for Sushma.

She had heard of him, *who hadn't?*

He was successful, had made his name in the accounting business. At one point, Suresh had dealt with Anand for approval of a loan needed for one of his commercial buildings. Suresh had like Anand and had said something about Anand's reputation for being very competent at his work. Sushma had never met him before and her brief meeting with him at the party made a strange impression on her.

When Sushma met him and said *"Namaste"* with folded hands, she was struck by the darkness hiding beyond the shiny pupils of his eyes. Sushma felt as if she was gazing into her own eyes. For a brief moment, the world had seemed to halt as they spoke briefly. She felt as if she needed to know more about him. Then, she saw a friend and excused herself to be part of the meaningless banter that would help her get through another evening. Another block of three hours filled, she thought. She caught his eye a couple of times during the evening and smiled at him. His gaze lingered on her a little longer, she thought. It was a slightly uncomfortable feeling and all along she knew that what she really, really wanted was a *drink*.

Thank God, it was Friday night. She did not have to worry about waking up to go to work in the morning. There were waiters carrying trays of beer and cheap champagne, and she was truly tempted to gulp down some champagne.

The evening wore on and Sushma grew restless. Her mind was preoccupied by how she could get a drink, without being seen. As a rule, she never drank in public. She grabbed a soft drink and the sweet sugary orange soda almost made her nauseated. She hid her nausea with a flashing smile as she quickly found the dinner buffet and made sure she ate some food. She made some more small talk with Anand when she saw that he was standing right next to her.

She remembered asking about his family and he mentioned something about his wife suffering from epilepsy. She was not sure that she even knew what epilepsy meant, but she shot a concerned and a sympathetic look at him. She murmured some concerning comments, trying to keep her hands steady as she placed some food into her plate. He placed a spoon onto her plate, and she looked up to thank him. Once again, she noticed the intense sadness that filled his eyes.

She wanted to find out more about him, but her craving for alcohol was so strong that she needed to run home. She could clearly visualize her bottle of whiskey; even remember the exact cupboard and shelf that it was on.

"He looks sad. Well, so what? The world is a sad place. I am sad too, perpetually and have been, for a long, long time" she said inwardly, hurrying away to her friends who had started their glorious gossip session.

She heard the meaningless talk, joined in with feigned interest and eventually muttered something polite and left the party as soon as her food was finished. She heaved a sigh of relief as she entered the sanctuary of her flat and hurried to the hidden cupboard, reaching for the prized bottle and poured herself a generous drink. That night she drank way more than she normally would, while she watched television, listening to meaningless Bollywood news and politics. It was way after midnight when she took another drink to make her doze off to sleep, right in her couch.

Her maid knocked at her door in the morning and gave her a deprecating look as she opened the door. The bottle was still open on the table. She wrinkled her nose as she picked up the bottle to put it away. She brought Sushma her cup of tea along with toast and started cleaning up.

"Bibi ji, do you know that Shanti babu has a small puppy dog now. My husband works in their house and says that he have to take the dog for a walk twice a day and his maid having to clean the whole house twice a day. There is so much hair in the house and my husband hates the smell of the dog."

"Ah, the water is so low pressure today. The committee people do nothing about the water, do they?"

"Hunh, there is no light in the bathroom. The bulb is fuse."

"What do you want me cook for lunch?"

Sushma welcomed her constant chatter. She still had a headache. She downed her aspirin with a glass of orange juice.

Her maid was cooking her favorite daal and was going to make rice and chapatti. She showered, changed and read the newspaper. As she went to switch the TV on again, a thought struck her head.

Maybe, she should get a dog!

She asked her maid to find out where Shanti babu got the dog from. The maid almost had a heart attack.

"No, no bibiji. No dog.
It is too too much trouble.
So dirty and the smell and the hair!
You would not like bibiji."

The next week Sushma brought home Suzy; a four-week-old Pomeranian. She was tempted to name it *Whiskey*, but good sense prevented her from doing that.

With time, Suzy became an extension of Sushma's life. For a while, Suzy replaced the need for alcohol and got Sushma away from the mindless drinking.

Sushma took Suzy for a walk in the park twice a day. Suzy was easy to train and soon started occupying Sushma's vacant life. Her antics kept Sushma entertained. She was thankful for the companionship. She talked to her in her special *Suzy* language. Much to her maid's disapproval; the dog ate at the table during dinner and slept at her feet when she watched tv.

Thanks to Suzy, Sushma's life had become livable to some extent.

CHAPTER

FIFTY ONE

THERE IS NO LIGHT IN THE DARK . . . 1981

Anand soon turned into a fascination for Sushma. He visited her office frequently on one pretext or the other. He could easily have sent one of his employees to take care of the required paperwork. He was awkward, always smiling more than needed and attempting to make pleasant conversation at the cost of appearing silly.

At some level, Sushma found the attention paid by Anand extremely flattering and enjoyable. She smiled at him and talked about inconsequential things. Her mind, though, was preoccupied with the urge to reach into her purse and take a drink from her flask that held her secret supply of alcohol.

Sushma was just starting to quit from her five years of drinking.

Still, she carried that flask with her just in case she started having tremors, or God forbid, hallucinations. She had read about the ugliness of alcohol withdrawals. She did not want anyone at work to see her going through the *shakes*. The absent-minded coy look that Anand saw on her face camouflaged her physical and psychological struggle to just open the flask and take a swig or two.

Slowly, with a lot of determination, Sushma was able to resist the craving. Each passing day, the flask in the purse grew more and more insignificant in her thoughts. After about six months, she was sober.

Sushma started to take interest in Anand and tried to find more about him. He was well known in the community. He was rich, successful and *married*. His wife was rarely seen. He had a grown son. He headed a successful accounting company. His son was in New Delhi.

When Sushma met Anand's wife, Kanta, at a common friend's party, she could not help but like her. Kanta talked to her at length, almost latching on to her as a long-lost best friend. Sushma felt genuine sadness when Kanta mentioned her disease and how it had overshadowed her life.

Unfortunately, that same night, upon reaching home, Sushma lapsed into drinking again. The very next morning, though, she swore to never touch the stuff again (as she had done many times before) and started the process of trying to give up drinking again.

CHAPTER
FIFTY TWO

YOU WILL HAVE TO SUFFER
AS WELL . . .

Kunal had found out where Sushma auntie lived. He had already visited her twice at her house.

He could smell the stench of alcohol as soon as he entered her house. She had her maid prepare coffee for Kunal. They sat in her drawing room and she enquired about Kanta. Kunal could barely get the words out of his mouth. Kanta was not doing well, was dying and it was only a matter of time.

It was easy for Sushma to see that Kunal was overcome with worry and grief. Occasionally, she saw an accusing look in his eyes, and she could not decipher the reason for that. She had only been helpful to Kanta.

Kunal saw the new puppy in Sushma's house. Suzy was a cute little creature that Sushma claimed was very perceptive and more intelligent than normal dogs. She had given Sushma auntie a purpose to live as after her husband's death she had been very lonely.

After about a half hour, Kunal thanked her for the coffee and left her house, promising to stay in touch and keep Sushma auntie informed about his mother's condition.

He could see that Suzy truly made Sushma auntie very happy.

Kunal vowed to himself, "Suzy would not stay alive very long."

Sushma had met Kunal when he came to see Kanta in the hospital. On their first meeting, he let Sushma know that he was happy that his mother had a friend and a caretaker.

She could see that Kunal was worried about his mother. He had an almost bitter expression on his face every time Kanta was hospitalized. He was starting to look older than his twenty-one years and Sushma could tell that he was drinking much more than Anand thought he did.

"It takes one to know one!"

Kunal was always polite and respectful towards her. Occasionally, he offered to drop her off at her home from the hospital. Once, she had invited him inside and had offered him a cup of coffee as he looked tired and drained. He saw her husband's picture and had politely enquired about him. He met Suzy and played with her briefly, stroking her fuzzy head. She asked him about his friends and his studies at the DAC and he answered her questions in an obligatory monotone. There was a brief moment during that conversation that Sushma thought she saw a look of longing in his eyes when he spoke of his friends. She thought that he wanted to tell her more, but in a flash that moment was gone. His eyes were covered with the same brooding, listless look that she sometimes saw in Anand's eyes.

The night before Kanta's death, she saw Kunal at the hospital during her visit. He looked haggard, as if he had not slept for a few nights. Anand had told her that Kunal was visiting and about Kunal's refusal to stay at home and that he had been staying at his friend's house.

"Hello, Kunal beta. How are you?"

"I am fine."

She noticed that he had not looked her in the eye. She tried to touch his arm as if to console him and he stayed stiff, unmoving in his chair.

"Beta, can I get you a cup of coffee from the cafeteria?"

"No, thank you."

She patted his shoulder and he held her hand in his and seemed to not want to let go. It was a strange grip, as if her hand was clenched in tentacles of an angry beast. He looked at her as if he was accusing her of something unforgivable. His look was so chilling that she felt herself shudder slightly.

The very next morning she learned that Kanta had died during the night.

That evening, Sushma was walking Suzy in the park. Her mind kept going to the last time she had seen Kanta and she could not forget the way Kunal had held on to her hand. She remembered his chilling glare that had raised so many questions in her mind.

She came out of the park and started walking to her car. Suzy was running ahead of her and trying to cross the road.

Suddenly, a red FIAT sped right in front of her, leaving her screaming at the top of her voice in anger. The very next moment Suzy lay on her back in a pool of blood, lifeless and whimpering, drawing her last few breaths in agony.

The car sped away, and she thought she saw a bearded face behind the wheel. It all happened too fast for her to even register the events in real time.

Her Suzy was gone and lay in a bloody shape at her feet.

Sushma did not see Anand for months after that. She had heard rumors that Kunal had a mental breakdown after his mother's death and had to be hospitalized after he attempted to attack Anand with a knife. Undoubtably these accounts were exaggerated versions of the real story, embellished animatedly by the person *(usually her cleaning lady)* that told her the story.

After Kanta's death, Anand and Sushma saw each other once at a charity dinner. His face was withered by grief. None of them made any effort to talk to each other. Wordlessly, with a subtle nod to Sushma, Anand turned to speak to the person shaking his hand.

Kanta's death was tangible throughout the evening; it took the form of an invisible fire that consumed their unnamed relationship, reducing it to ashes.

That very evening, Sushma put her apartment up for sale and made arrangements to move to her hometown to pursue teaching in a small private school.

She did not call Anand or leave a forwarding address.

CHAPTER

FIFTY THREE

MAYA . . . 2018

"It was so school girlish, was it not?" she thought to herself.

Falling in love with Kunal's brooding eyes that hid crazed thoughts, a head of disheveled hair that disguised a monster, a heart that hid a gory mystery; only an infatuated schoolgirl would have failed to detect his diabolical nature. His moodiness and suspicious nature seemed to make sense now. When Maya tried to think back, Kunal's behavior had certainly deteriorated after he found out about her affair.

She felt guilty for a brief second.

"Did I cause his insanity?"

She had sought counseling, she had apologized, she had changed herself. After her brief escapades, she had been nothing but a devoted wife and mother. Her mind quickly rationalized her guilt away.

Her phone rang and Kunal's counselor was on the phone. He wanted Maya to meet him urgently in his office, he emphasized *"as soon as possible."*

He sounded concerned, panicked even.

Maya drove to his office, forcing herself to be calm and pay attention to the traffic. Her mind was not able to formulate any thoughts and she needed some guidance on how to proceed. Her main concern was her safety and Sonu's protection.

The office was crowded. Patients were waiting in the crowded waiting room. The office staff led her to his office, and she waited in the chair forcing herself from peeling her nail paint with her nails, a bad habit that surfaced in times of severe anxiety.

As the doctor entered the room and sat down, she looked at him across the desk.

"Well," he said. *"I am glad you are here. At present, Mr. Sinha, is taking his medications and is following up with his appointments. He is functioning well and is managing his business well. He says that he truly loves you and wants to take care of you. He has expressed no suicidal or homicidal thoughts".*

"The reason I wanted to contact you was because of some new information that came up during his last session, which was late last evening. I wanted you to know about something that happened in the past. Last night, during his session, he admitted to killing his mother by injecting her with a large dose of potassium chloride, while she lay on her deathbed in the hospital. He insists that he did it to save her from ongoing misery.

He also attacked his father and stabbed him repeatedly with a knife before his mother passed away. He particularly relished recounting the incident of how he killed a dog that belonged to a woman his father was having an affair with. These events happened more than 35 years ago."

Maya could not stop shaking. Beads of sweat rapidly crowded her forehead. She was surprised to know that the man she had fallen for, slept with and borne a child with was a *murderer!*

Maya found her voice and impatiently bombarded him with questions.

"Did the doctor not have any responsibility in the matter for protecting them?"

"Could Kunal not turn violent towards her and Sonu unexpectedly?"

"Shouldn't he be committed to a mental institution?"

The doctor answered calmly.

"I understand your concern and your worry. However, I want to point out what I had mentioned earlier. At present, Mr. Sinha, is taking his medications and is following up with his appointments. He has expressed no suicidal or homicidal thoughts. He has not committed a crime and I genuinely feel that he is not a threat to your safety."

Maya was overcome with panic and found it hard to think straight. How should she protect herself and Sonu? What would she tell him? What should she do next?

She called her lawyer who suggested that she should definitely inform her son of her concerns.

Maya called Sonu from the phone in the doctor's office. Sonu's disbelief was apparent. He tried to joke about it saying that she was overreacting.

"You really need to chill, Mom. Obviously, things are not as bad as you are trying to make it sound."

She made the doctor speak directly to Sonu on the phone, urging him to be careful.

After she hung up the phone with Sonu, Maya decided to leave town and move away, far away from Kunal. She definitely could not go on living under the same roof after knowing what she knew now. She could imagine Kunal's hooded eyes hiding crazed thoughts of violence following her everywhere.

Even if the doctor did not think so, she believed that Kunal was dangerous. He had probably received the notice for divorce by now. Maya could palpably sense the violence of his backlash and was truly scared for her life.

She called the police from the doctor's office. She was very terrified and did not want to go back to the house by herself.

The policeman let her know *(with a jeer!)* that no crime had been committed *yet*. They were not going to *"arrest"* Kunal, just because she thought that he should be arrested. He encouraged her to come down to the station and lodge a report so that he could discuss with his boss and take necessary steps *(according to protocol)*. He suggested that she should move out of the house and be with a friend for the next few days until she felt safe.

Maya had never been more frightened in her life.

She called Devyani and asked her to help her.

She called Sonu again and asked him to promise to be careful and not come home until everything was sorted out.

Devyani called her back and said that she had booked her a hotel room for a week. She insisted that Maya should stay with her for the night.

"Thank God for Devyani," Maya thought.

She called her lawyer's office again. She asked them to arrange for someone to accompany her to her house so that she could bring her belongings to the hotel room. The firm asked for an *additional* fee for that, which she reluctantly agreed to pay.

They sent a young male intern to drive with her to her house.

Maya entered her house, frightened and sad at the same time. She checked the garage and was relieved to see that Kunal's car was not in the garage: he was probably at work. She wanted to collect her things and leave as soon as possible.

One last look at the world they had created together, the designer furniture, the eclectic art collection, her favorite chinaware, her Royal Albert tea service, the dirty dishes in the sink. Every little thing made her heart sad and tears were streaming down her face. Through blurred eyes she started packing a suitcase.

The intern waited in the car in the driveway, immersed in his cell phone. He did not see Kunal park his car two houses away and walk into the house through the back entrance.

Maya was still folding her clothes when she heard the backdoor open. Her heart leapt into her mouth and pounded fiercely. She heard Kunal's footsteps and tried not to scream. He entered the living room quickly climbing the stairs up to her room. His footsteps were now getting closer to her.

Through the window Maya could see the intern, seated in his car, still engrossed in his cell phone. She reached for her phone and dialed 911 and screamed for help when the operator picked up the phone.

Kunal was at her door now.

Maya could see the stainless-steel blade of her favorite kitchen knife; the handle clasped tightly in his clenched fist. Rays of sunlight danced off from the shiny metal and split into a rainbow of colors. She was oddly mesmerized with the shining blade, as it got closer to her at a steady pace. She looked up briefly and saw the expression of utter hatred outlining Kunal's face.

In the next few seconds, her thoughts were merely brief segments of pain.

A brutal force, a slicing noise as the blade cut through her chest wall, a blinding throbbing pain exploding through her lungs, unstopping, her own voice mangled by screams, the sound of the knife dropping onto the floor, until there was ____darkness.

Kunal gazed at the fast collecting pool of blood on the floor, mesmerized by the rich red tones of the liquid. Calmly, he retrieved his cell phone from his pocket and called Sonu. As usual, his son did not pick up the phone and it annoyed Kunal. He had to leave a message.

"Sonu, this is Dad. Mom has had a slight accident. When are you coming, beta?"

As if in slow motion, Kunal looked through the window. It was an unusually sunny day. The mildly tinted window filtered out the bright sunlight. He could hear a police siren in the distance getting closer and closer. The noise was rudely jarring to his ears. Kunal saw the young intern look back at the police cars which were rapidly arriving at his house. Three officers were at his door, with their guns drawn. They did not wait for him to answer the door. They broke down his door and as if in a second, they were in the room. They were reading him his rights as they handcuffed him and led him out to the police vehicle. Kunal looked back at his house with a confused look. The police siren started again, deafening him.

THE END

.